T0164713

Give Some Take More

IS BLOOD THICKER THAN WATER

A NOVEL BY SCHERELL SIMONET

 www.trafford.com

North America & international
toll-free: 1 888 232 4444 (USA & Canada)
phone: 250 383 6864 ♦ fax: 812 355 4082

Dedication

This book is dedicated to my biggest fans, Fred, Patrell and Kiana. Thank you for being the best husband and daughters any wife and mother could ever ask for. Without your love, patience and support, this book would not have been possible.

To my mother, Mandlyn Williams, thank you for having me. You are a fine example of a role model for young single mothers who strive to instill courage, strong values and determination in their children who must fight to succeed when all the odds are against them.

Also, to nine strong and courageous women:

Kioka R. Broussard, Brittany Hebert, Keisha Celestand, Summer Walker
Lindsey Hernandez, Erin Rode-Fiorello, Karen Gibbs, Linda Lentz and Debora Tremont

Sometimes we all need words of encouragement to help us along the way. You all are great counselors. Continue touching the hearts of others just as you've touched mine. Thank you for being my inspiration.

Acknowledgements

Ladies of Essence Book Club of Baton Rouge, Louisiana.

Thanks so much for welcoming me to Baton Rouge with open arms. Words cannot express how much you all mean to me. You are my sisters.

Charron Thomas, Sanettria Glasper-Pleasant, Kelli K. Dixon, N. Manuel, Rolanda M. Durham-Gros, Antonya Coleman-Crump, Christa Davis, Deidra M. Douglas, Davetta Nelson, Jean Dorsey Martin, Towanda Taylor, Carondalette Rogers, Siminola Pavageau and Dawn Mellion-Patin

Special Thanks to: Jeanne C. Warren, Kendra Toodle-Register, Rhonda Brooks, Roshell Jones and my Auntie Gina for being the first eyes to read my work in progress. I know your ears are still tired from listening to my venting on countless occasions. Thanks to "The PaperBoyz," Kiandre Gillespie and Mike Charles. Thanks to my cousin, Trevor Foster at "Tru Books"and to my cousin, NaDariah Gillespie, the baddest cosmetician on the East Coast. Brian Fontenot, my editor, thanks for all of your support. Last but not least, thanks to models, Breonne Hall and Patrell Mckenzie for allowing me to put your beautiful faces on my cover.

Prologue

I could smell the gun powder and see the smoke circulating through the air after the bullet exited the barrel. I was just seven and I had to use a couple of my fingers when I pulled the trigger on the gun my father kept under the bed in a shoe box I was forbidden to touch. But I felt it was a good time for me to use it.

The sirens from the police cruisers echoed outside of the living room window. The blue and red lights brightly lit up the street. It drowned out the glare from the pole lights that children depended on to remind them of curfew. My mother stood in the middle of the floor holding her head. Her body rapidly shook. The blood dripped from her forehead, through her fingers, and onto the beige linoleum floor. My father decided to give her a beating with his fist after giving her previous warnings against allowing her brother, Charm, to interfere with taking care of his family. My father wasn't handling his responsibility but didn't want anyone else doing it for him. My mother was being defiant. She wanted her children to have the best of everything. My father despised it. He slept with other women and took care of their children instead of his own. When he realized my mother wasn't a needy case, she became his punching bag. I'd had enough. I was sure she was fed up, too.

My younger sister, Chenoa, was four at the time. Her pink pajamas were soiled with red stains from the blood that was also splattered on the walls. She sat in the corner of the room with her hands covering her face. She peeked through them with terror at my father's limp body lying on the floor next to her. The blood drained from his forehead like my mother's but his came from a bullet wound.

I heard loud voices coming from the outside hallway of our building. The police were coming to get me. I was startled by the pounding at the steel door. I threw the gun down. My mom hesitated but managed to open the door. It was my uncle Charm and his friend. They must have come in through the back entrance of the building. They hurried inside of our house. They didn't bother asking what happened. They saw my father's body lying dead on the floor. My uncle's friend scooped up Chenoa. Uncle charm lifted me up next. I felt safe. They carried us out of the house. My mother trailed behind them. When we exited the front entrance of the building, all of the sirens were off but the lights were blinding. With guns pointed, the police yelled, "Come out slowly with your hands up!"

Chenoa
Chapter One

Baller's Territory

Mr. Smith, my English teacher, looked like he probably worked out maybe twice a day, which I found quite impressive for a man his age. He was balding, short, and stocky. It seemed he always made sure to smell nice just in case a desperate student decided to make an appointment to get up close and personal or do whatever was necessary to tease his suppressed male ego to get his attention. I'm not a cologne connoisseur, but I think he was wearing the same Old Spice Cologne my grandfather used to wear. I always liked the smell, especially when my grandfather used to wear it the few times he visited my sister, Deloris, and me.

After weeks of falling behind in my English class, I decided to check my grade. I had a D, which was still a passing grade. I needed at least a B in order to get into the university I wanted to attend instead of going to the community college in my town. I wanted to be introduced to new experiences, meet new people, and live a different life. Being the first in my family to attend a four-year university and graduate with honors was important to me. But judging by the direction I was heading, I wondered if I was going to make it out of high school.

Mr. Smith knew I was in trouble inside and outside of his class. He knew I had Demetri, my son, who was two. I hadn't received any help from his father, Lance. I completely trusted that man with my heart. The last time I saw him was when I told him I was pregnant.

Once the class cleared, Mr. Smith motioned for me to come over to his desk. Before coming over, I decided to leave my book bag on my chair. My books were already packed away for the day, so I figured I would grab it on the way out. He wanted to speak with me about earning some extra credit. I visited the writing center in the past faithfully but had issues with finding a dedicated tutor to help me. Mr. Smith said my writing skills were weak, but when they read my papers, it seemed they had difficulty with finding the problem. I wasn't sure if their time was being wasted or mine. It seemed the tutors didn't want to speak against Mr. Smith. He might have helped them get their jobs.

At the center, I believe the tutors were dishonest. They made deals under the table for their own benefit. The free one-hour sessions became costly because the tutors only offered limited assistance. Once they found out the severity of the writing problems students were having, they began determining the amount to charge per minute, after exhausting the free one-hour service. The school was already paying the tutors by the hour, but they wanted more money. For some strange reason, I needed more than an hour. I knew my pockets couldn't handle their fees. I began realizing then to be on the lookout when I saw the word, "free." Every time I saw it, there was some scam involved.

Mr. Smith's eyes scanned my body from head to toe, as I sat in the desk next to his. This was actually a good dress day for me. Because I was feeling so bummed out about my English grade, I decided to dress up so I could look good on the outside, even though I was disappointed and felt like I was letting myself down. I thought it might cheer me up. So, I wasn't wearing the usual faded jeans with whatever top found my finger tips first. I wore a cute black mini dress I found on sale at Macy's

Department Store. The dress wasn't anything special, but for me it was definitely a change. My shoes weren't a name brand, just a pair of black Payless leather pumps, so I hoped no one noticed I only paid ten dollars for them. I liked the shoes mostly because of the straps. They crossed in the front then circulated around my ankles to help support them. They reminded me of a pair of sandals worn by one of the female mistresses on a gladiator series I watched.

I felt good about my sudden change in appearance until third hour. By then, I became annoyed with my hair and decided to pull it back into its usual ponytail. Due to the lack of attention paid to it, my hair grew a few inches over the years. My hair didn't have any natural body. I tried wearing it out, but whenever I held my head down to write, it flopped in the way. In the mornings I didn't have much time to work with it anyway. Along with dressing Demetri, doing my hair became a struggle, so I didn't see why black people made such a fuss about having long hair.

I sat in Mr. Smith's hot seat, waiting for him to say something. He just stared at me.

"Chenoa, you look absolutely gorgeous today," he said with a slight stutter.

Nervous from Mr. Smith's compliment, my palms and underarms started to sweat.

"Thank you," I replied, sensing he was getting ready to say some inappropriate things, because of the way his tongue kept licking his upper lip.

"A beautiful girl like yourself is quite the distraction for me. Because of you, I frequently lose my concentration and have to find my place in my lesson plan."

He smiled and patted my knee, making me tense up and shift my body to one side. I crossed my legs then looked at the picture of his wife on his desk. After that, I just wanted to get out of there. I figured I was wasting my time with him when I should have been concerned about the time, because missing my bus was not an option. Catching the school bus was the only way home for Demetri and me. I wanted to interrupt Mr. Smith, while he was still rambling, but I waited patiently until he passed the complimentary stage of his conversation.

As he continued, he asked me a question that had nothing to do with English. He wanted to know how I spent my spare time. I told him I enjoyed going to the movies. I knew I'd told a lie, because I did not have any time to spare. And he was aware I was a single mother, so most of my time was devoted to my son. He then asked for my phone number. Not once did he offer any help or show any concern as to why I was averaging a D in his class. I wondered if he was willing to help me with my work or if he expected me to grant some type of sexual favor to earn the grade I needed. Why did he want my phone number and what difference did my extracurricular activities or hobbies make? I felt nervous not knowing what to expect. And, because his rambling worsened, I was left with no other choice but to push our meeting along.

To avoid missing my bus, I wrote down my cell phone number and handed it to him after recording his number in my phone. My dress didn't have any pockets, so I placed my cell phone on his desk. I didn't feel comfortable with walking back to my desk to place my phone in my bag. Besides, I had a bus to catch. My goal was to continue walking out of his classroom.

My purpose for giving Mr. Smith my number was simply to stop him from talking. He didn't offer any advice on how I could improve my grade. I wasn't sure what he had up his sleeve, but I hoped this unexpected get-together had nothing to do with sex if he decided to call. I couldn't figure out how I would make myself available to him anyway. I didn't have anyone to watch Demetri, especially at the drop of a hat. Any "me" time was totally out of the question, unless Deloris had some spur of the moment event she wanted to take Demetri to. But with my bad luck, I wasn't expecting a break anytime soon.

I tried not thinking about Mr. Smith's comments, but couldn't ignore his unwanted voice in my head and the disgusting thought of even forcing myself to see him any other way other than as my English teacher. When I looked back while walking out of his class, his eyes were locked on my ass.

When I finally got to Demetri, the late bell already rung, so I knew the school daycare was closing. The other children had already left with their mothers. Demetri's teacher, Ms. Johnson, rolled her eyes the minute I walked through her classroom door. She looked tired. She stood over Demetri as he sat on the special rug she normally allowed the children to sit on only during story time. She was eight months pregnant but her pregnancy wasn't very noticeable since she was normally so heavy set. I assumed she must have been on her feet all day, chasing after toddlers, because her feet were bare and swollen. Demetri took to her well. I was a bit concerned because her replacement while on maternity leave was scheduled to take over in a week. Usually, Ms. Johnson would give a report on Demetri's progress for the day, but I only remember hearing the sound of her teeth sucking to let me know she was not happy. When Demetri looked up and saw me, he stood up, ran to the toy box, and threw the red toy car he had been playing with inside the box. I thanked Ms. Johnson, grabbed Demetri's bag from the floor, quickly scooped him up, and then dashed out of the school just in time to see we missed our bus.

For a winter's day in Hartford, Connecticut, it was beautiful, but hot. It must have been eighty five degrees, but I wasn't getting my hopes up. I was well aware that the sun would be playing hide go seek soon.

My stomach hurt and I was exhausted from running with Demetri. I put him down and held his hand, so he wouldn't run off. I needed time to think. Not having a dime in my pocket was a problem, especially when I needed to figure out a way for us to get home. Deloris didn't live far from the school. I knew she wouldn't have a problem with coming to get us. When I reached in my bag to get my cell phone, I couldn't feel it next to any of the other things I had thrown inside, so I let go of Demetri's hand and took another look. This time, I searched Demetri's bag, too. After digging around for a few minutes, I realized I'd left my phone on Mr. Smith's desk. I was almost sure he had left for the day unless he was meeting with another student about earning extra credit points. I wasn't going back to his classroom to find out. I figured the main office would still be open. I would use the phone there to call my sister and get my cell phone from him some other time.

I didn't want to think about the office being closed. The only other available phone to use would have been the pay phone inside of the cafeteria. I didn't have any money, not even change to use the pay phone. My welfare check wasn't due for a few days. I regretted quitting my waitressing job, but couldn't afford paying for child care. All of the money I made from waitressing went to the babysitter. After school every day, I would work my part-time waitressing job at a little café downtown to try to cover the childcare expense. I needed childcare during school hours so I could continue going and graduate. I would have loved to continue working if I didn't have to pay for child care. Thankfully, the high school I attended began offering onsite childcare during school hours. This was a service for young mothers who pursued earning their high school diplomas with the intent of attending college. I was interested in going to college, but didn't have any idea what I wanted to major in. The Child Development Department made it possible for mothers like me to finish school and earn college credit, but only if we were interested in majoring in Early Childhood Education, so I told them anything so I could finish. I needed to seriously think about a major because I didn't have the time or the money to waste for exploring, not with my responsibilities.

While standing outside getting ready to go back inside of the school, someone yelled, "Chenoa!"

I barely recognized the voice. It belonged to my cousin, Trinity, who was a junior, a year behind me. She was potentially pretty, but she did not have anything going for her in the feminine department. Her sexuality was always in question. She had long hair that reached the mid section of her spine, which she wore corn rowed back. It was a style usually worn by girls that were athletes, inmates, expecting mothers, or someone maybe anticipating on getting into a fight. This style was solely for the purpose of avoiding any unnecessary hair distraction. As a matter of fact, Laila Ali wore this hairstyle during her boxing matches. I guess this hairstyle could have worked for me too, but when I was a little girl, I hated wearing braids.

Along with the corn rows, Trinity had a piercing in her left eyebrow and one in the middle of the lining of her bottom lip. The rings she wore in them were gold studs. She had dark skin that she tattooed with the permission of her mother. Her name was written around her upper arm and Mickey Mouse was located on her thigh. They were barely noticeable. I only noticed her tattoos when she came to school half dressed to show them off. I'm not sure if she was half naked because she wanted the girls to see them, or the boys. I don't think she had any insecurity with her body. She lived at the gym. She pumped so much iron and burned so many calories she lost her boobs, and her flat chest didn't match the rump that her mother gave her.

But Trinity should have been glad her mother gave her something!

Her mother, my Aunt Pooler, was nuttier than a fruit cake. She would start fights then somehow inch her way out of them. Before knowing it, people would be fighting one another without knowing the reason behind the fight. One thing I could say, Aunt Pooler knew how to play pool, which was how she received her nickname. She had skills and would hustle anybody just for the hell of it. She chain smoked cigarettes and spent hours at the pool room playing some of the best players in town and some of the best players from out of town that traveled just to challenge her. But then, a fight would break out or the police would raid the place. It's funny how she would end up being seen at other places, other than in jail, where her opponents were brought.

Aunt Pooler was also a very jealous person. She never wanted to see anyone have more than her or even liked seeing anyone else happy. With her, it was all about competition. Being competitive was one thing, but

Aunt Pooler took competing to another level. No one could stand her. I know I couldn't.

I remembered listening to the stories my mother used to tell. Ever since Aunt Pooler was a little girl, she had this jealousy problem. On Christmas Day, when she and my mother were young, Aunt Pooler would throw the biggest tantrums after opening her toys that Santa left. She threw fits because she liked the toys Santa left for my mother better. She would complain if the baby doll my mother held in her arms had something more, even something as simple as one extra layer of lace on its dress than her baby doll. She would then snatch the baby doll from my mother's arms and deliberately pull the head off.

Trinity inherited some of those same ways from her mother. Even though my cousin Trinity and I got along when were kids, when we grew up, we realized we weren't as close anymore. But, we still tried working at our relationship by hanging out every now and then. Our hangouts often ended on bad notes. Trinity had her friends but most people didn't like dealing with her. She was jealous, devious, and trifling, which was why she was called Trinity. Her negative characteristics appeared in threes.

"Yo Chenoa, what chu doin wit dat boy out heah in da hot sun like dat?"

I don't know why she chose to always use Ebonics when she spoke. I knew better. She always wanted everyone to think she was down. Trinity was the smartest student in her class. Trinity made perfect grades and her mother made sure everyone knew it. She made sure to send a copy of the Honor Roll with her name on it to all of our family members every semester to ensure that we did not get it twisted. She wanted everyone to know which granddaughter she thought had the most potential of succeeding.

"Demetri and I missed our bus," I said.

"Girl, don't worry bout it! My girl, Nikki'll give y'all a ride home." Trinity said.

"Are you sure," I asked. "I don't have any money to pay for gas? Who is your friend Nikki?"

"Ya' know her," she answered. "She used to go wit Uncle Pop."

Our Uncle Pop was about five years older than me, so I questioned why Trinity would be hanging out with someone who dated him. He was my mother's youngest brother. He was the only one in our family to show interest with attending the armed forces. After he graduated from high school, he took the entrance exam to join the Navy. When he passed it, his interest became a reality. He was the laughing stock of the community. Joining the military was considered the worse thing a black man could do, especially from the projects. His friends asked him why he wanted to fight the white man's war, when there was a war to fight here, everyday, in our own neighborhood. They had a point! Every time I turned around, there was somebody getting stabbed, shot, or killed. My guess would be he thought he was going to escape violence by enlisting into the Navy. But after making it through basic training and living on base for a few months, it was time for him to go to war. He began having trouble breathing and was diagnosed with asthma. His symptoms worsened every time he participated in a drill, so the military sent him back home. He was probably still the laughing stock of the neighborhood, but while others were laughing, he was cashing his veteran's disability check at the bank every month. Ever since, he was known as Pop.

When Nikki pulled up, Trinity pretty much told her she was giving Demetri and me a ride home without asking. By the look on Nikki's face, she didn't seem pleased knowing she would be carrying an extra load. I liked the car she was driving. I think it was a new silver BMW 745i. Instantly, I wondered if it belonged to her. I was desperate for a ride and all, but I wanted to know what she did for a living that would allow her to afford such an expensive car. She wasn't working the cash register at Wal-Mart—that's for sure—and I didn't want to be involved in any illegal activity that would get me thrown in jail. But then I figured, knowing her business wouldn't make much of a difference. I was just getting a quick ride home anyway.

Before getting inside of the car, I tried remembering if I recognized Nikki. She wasn't someone I recalled dating Uncle Pop. She really didn't seem like Uncle Pop's type. He used to like dark girls with meat on their bones; she was very thin and light skinned and had dark big round eyes that sort of reminded me of Olive Oil from Popeye. My uncle and Popeye surely had a few things in common.

After getting inside of the car, Nikki periodically glanced at me through her rearview mirror. My uncle was probably attracted to her full lips, which covered a set of beautiful pearly white teeth. I noticed them mostly from her reflection through the rear view mirror when she spoke, because she didn't crack a smile the whole time we were in the car. I figured she kept looking in her rearview mirror to make sure Demetri wasn't spilling anything from the sippy cup I gave him before getting inside. Her leather seats were plush and her new carpet was screaming for a two-year-old to stain it.

On the way home listening to Trinity and Nikki's conversation, Nikki seemed really agitated with a girl named Rhonda. Rhonda was making passes at her new boyfriend, Jay, during a basketball game they went to last week. And she wanted Rhonda to know who Jay belonged to.

I hadn't been to a basketball game since freshman year, since having Demetri. I wondered if she was talking about a college basketball game, because I couldn't imagine her talking about a high school game. Why would she want to hang around a bunch of teenagers at a high school game? But then again, Trinity was still in high school. She was also closer with Uncle Pop than me. She probably developed a close bond with Nikki during the time they were dating.

Looking out of the window, I began paying closer attention to the different route Nikki was taking to my house after I'd given her directions. I wondered if she had trouble with following directions or if she just totally disregarded the possibility that I wanted to know where the driver was taking me. After looking at me again from her rearview mirror, she read the look on my face.

"Chenoa, do you mind if I make a quick stop," Nikki asked, staring at me through the mirror.

"No, I don't mind," I said.

"Good, I'm going to sneak up on his ass," she said. "I wanna see how much playing around he thinks he's going to do tonight."

"Wait, are you getting ready to drive to the basketball game?"

"Yeah, it's only gonna take a minute," she said. "I have to go to work in the morning, so I'm not trying to be out all night."

"Where do you work? This is really a nice car."

I waited for her answer. Trinity was quiet and looking out of the window.

"I work for BMW. I am a salesperson there. This is one of their loaners," she replied. "None of the customers needed to use this one today, so I signed it out to use for myself."

"How much does the game cost? I didn't bring any money with me," I lied, as I didn't have any to bring.

"Girl, you don't need no money," Trinity chimed in, as she stopped looking out of the window and then turned her body around toward my direction. "I got chu!"

Going to a basketball game wasn't part of my plan. I had mixed feelings, because Demetri was going to be thrown off his schedule and I suspected it was going to rain. I didn't want to be out in bad weather. But after giving it some thought, I didn't see any harm, especially when she mentioned she wasn't staying. I was getting a free ride home, so the weather wasn't really a factor. I decided to roll with them.

When we reached the game at the Civic Center, I could see this wasn't going to be just any usual high school basketball game. This game was the playoff between the two most popular colleges on the East Coast, University of Connecticut and Georgetown University. I was relieved because I was dressed my best, plus the wind hadn't taken over my hair, leaving my ponytail still neatly intact. I didn't have to worry about Demetri's appearance, either. If only I was prepared for the night I would have brought his stroller, because I wanted him to stay clean. Usually, his clothes were a mess by the end of the school day, but they weren't soiled, which was a change for him, too. The Polo Jeans, Red Pullover Polo Shirt, and Jordon Sneakers that my sister gave him made him look older than he was. His haircut was also nice and fresh. Because I hadn't taken care of my own hair, didn't mean I was neglecting Demetri's.

As we approached the building, the big sign posted in front of the stadium read, "Parking for Ballers." This must have been up Nikki's alley because she pulled right up to the curb. She wanted to be seen right in front of the building getting out of the new BMW she was borrowing. After we got out of the car, the valet parking attendants took her keys and the money from Nikki for the service. I saw the admirers hanging around, as if they were waiting to see if a celebrity was going to appear. A few of them wanted to know who I was. It seemed I was getting most of the attention, even though I was the backseat driver. I think that sort of pissed Trinity and Nikki off. I guess they wished they'd dropped me off first before coming to the game. By the way she pulled up to the curb in the Beemer, she struck me as the attention seeking type. The last thing I wanted to do was piss Nikki off and make her change her mind about giving us a ride home. I'm not really sure what was going through Trinity's head. She had a strange look on her face that reminded me of a look her jealous mother would have. Surprisingly, Demetri was still in the mood for walking. He was right by my side. I avoided making eye contact with any of the guys. I didn't want them thinking I was of the least bit interested, especially when I was going through an ordeal with taking care of a baby all by myself. I didn't have the time for any additional drama. I kept my attention focused on my son as I guided him toward the building with my hand placed on the back of his head.

As we walked toward the building, I could hear the moans and groans coming from male voices that carried in the unexpected wind. Then I heard a deep voice with a New York accent that I would recognize anywhere. I looked for him in the crowd, and his words became clearer.

"Man, y'all must be crazy, disrespecting my girl and my kid."

I stopped dead in my tracks, stood there, and then stared at the most beautiful man, the one I fell in love with. This was the man I'd given my virginity to and created a life with. This was the man who shattered me.

Lance looked great. He always had a nice body. His biceps were more pronounced than I remembered, which meant he was putting more time into taking care of himself than taking care of his son. I wondered which team he was supporting because the jersey he wore was blue, white and gray. Both teams wore blue, but the accent colors were white, which represented UCONN, and the gray, Georgetown. I wasn't surprised. Lance probably thought he was making a statement. He was probably there for the ladies and could care less about the game. He wore blue jeans that were loose fitted and a pair of tan, Timberland boots. He stood there smiling at us, as if he'd been there from the beginning of my son's life until then. He looked proud, as if he was trying to take credit for all of the sleepless nights I endured, while trying not to appear half dead when it came time for school the next day. Trying to put food in our mouths, keeping clothes on our backs, and holding everything else together at the same time, these things I did by myself, he took pride in. Did he forget?

"Hey Chenoa and Demetri," he called to us.

I didn't even think he knew his son's name.

Before I knew it, he had picked Demetri up and started kissing on him. Demetri was confused. He was probably wondering who the hell this person was, even though he was the spitting image of this stranger. He had his curly black hair, coffee brown complexion, and big golden hazel eyes, looking almost as if he could be of Indian descent. I used to have similar features when I was a baby. When my mother first saw me, she said I looked like a little Indian baby. She was determined to give me a Native American name, so the nurse suggested the name Chenoa. It meant white dove.

Lance asked if he could have a moment with me. I was very interested in hearing what he possibly had to say to me after all of the time that had passed. It was obvious he didn't want anybody to know the truth. This was the first time seeing his son. I didn't want to embarrass him by making a scene. He felt ashamed already, which was why he needed to put on a show when he saw us.

Lance still had a smooth demeanor, evidenced by the way he softly grabbed me by my waist with one hand and pulled me into a little corner giving us some privacy. He held Demetri's hand with the other. Nikki and Trinity told me they would meet me inside, as he pulled me away. They weren't going to get involved with a dispute or anything else involving my son's father and me. They paid for their tickets then walked inside after getting their hands stamped. I didn't know what I was thinking allowing myself to come to a basketball game without any money. I shouldn't have let them go inside without me. How was I supposed to pay to get in? I didn't want to say I was broke. Then I would have looked as if I didn't have myself together. I was too proud for that.

I could feel the tension in Lance's fingers as his right hand held onto my waist. I maneuvered my hips in such a way that forced him to let go of his grip. But, deep down inside, I missed his touch and wanted his hand to remain where it was. I wouldn't let him know that though. I felt weak and hated myself for it.

"Chenoa, I know I haven't been there for you and Demetri," he said. "I understand how much I probably put you both through by not coming around. I know you're probably wondering what kind of man would leave such a beautiful woman and his precious son like I have. I left you hanging and want to make it up to you, to the both of you. Let me at least invite you to come and sit with me in the skybox to watch the game. This will give us some time to talk. Then afterwards, if you allow me to bring y'all home, I can possibly start a relationship with my son before it's too late. I really do want him to know me."

I should have told him it would be a cold day in hell before I allowed him to just pop back into my life and call himself making anything up to us. Where the hell had he been? Didn't he know I was struggling trying to raise our son by myself? Was his ass really this crazy? Give me some damn money, instead. But, I looked into his eyes and melted. My body yearned to be with him. I knew my mind was playing tricks, but I was out of control. It felt good seeing him, seeing him smile at me, but I wanted to keep fighting my emotions. No matter how hard I tried, I couldn't win. I decided to take him up on his offer.

When we approached the door, Lance grabbed and flashed a card that was attached to a lanyard around his neck. As we walked inside of the building, several females rolled their eyes at me. At first, I hoped it wasn't because they noticed my Payless Shoes, but I still strutted because I was with my son and his father. What more could a girl ask for than to make a public appearance with the man she always loved and the son who was the spitting image of his father.

Deloris
Chapter Two

Duck, Duck, Goose

O n my way to the nail shop, the clouds were getting thick. I could barely see the sun. It was Thursday, so instead of sitting in the parlor all day on Friday or Saturday, I beat the weekend rush.

When I arrived, I was not in any mood for listening to the two Vietnamese ladies joke and laugh in their language. I couldn't understand what the hell they were talking about, and I had a problem with that, especially since I was paying them five hundred dollars a month for manicures and pedicures. I didn't like the idea of them talking bad about me, being that I was their most loyal and generous customer.

While sitting in the chair, I looked out of the window, hoping the rain would hold off until after I reached home. I hated when the polish on my toes smudged because I rushed out to get home or it got wet in the rain. I was planning to babysit my nephew Demetri for a few hours this weekend. My sister, Chenoa, was going through a rough time with school and trying to take care of him, but I rarely felt sorry for her. She brought all of that shit on herself. Knowing our family's financial pull, she should have known better. She didn't have to struggle to pay for no damn milk for Demetri.

Before we were even born, our uncle Charm formed one of the toughest gangs in Connecticut. Because of him, our family was secure when it came to wanting or needing for anything. He even helped others within the community by sponsoring functions to raise money for families in need. And because of our uncle, my sister and I always had the best of everything, so that struggling shit Chenoa was going through was no friend of mine. As a matter of fact, I didn't even know it. I can remember when we were little girls. We rode around the projects all day long on a variety of Power Wheels Jeeps, Corvettes, and Buggies. We drove whatever we wanted whenever we wanted. But when she got older, she wanted to catch the damn city bus? The way I saw it, riding the city bus just meant you were either broke or too damn scared to get a driver's license. And if either were the case, you didn't need to be on the road anyhow. I didn't know what was wrong with Chenoa, but I was driving a candy apple red Jaguar given to me by Uncle Charm. Now keeping it real, I was the first born female from his older sister and was truly his princess.

Chenoa and I were three years apart. I was very mature, sometimes too mature for my own good. I always felt I knew what was best for me. A quality I didn't think my sister had. Uncle Charm and the gang didn't have to worry about me as much. One Love was the name of the gang. In the black community, One Love was another way for acknowledging the closeness of a friendship. The friendship was bonded and considered similar to a biological connection of a blood relative. We liked to think of the gang as a brotherhood. All of the members were really like family, even if my grandmother didn't carry them in her womb.

The gang was looked upon as a positive organization for our neighborhood. On the flip side of things, when other gangs threatened our community, One Love showed no mercy when it came to protecting it. The media only exposed the negative aspects of the gang, so outsiders had difficulty understanding its purpose and how One Love contributed to the community.

I could say we had happy childhoods, but growing up it was difficult for us to date. One Love was a bit overprotective of Chenoa and me when it came to having boyfriends. This could be one of the reasons she never told anyone who Demetri's father was. She knew if Uncle Charm found out about punk ass Lance before getting pregnant, there was no telling what would have happened to him. I bet she prayed every night to the Good Lord that I wouldn't spill the beans. She didn't have anything to worry about, though. Uncle Charm had already given Lance a pass. He figured the damage was already done and didn't want to leave his great nephew without a father. I knew this much, though. Had I heard that Lance mistreated Chenoa or my nephew, other than staying away, I would have been ready to kill his ass myself for hurting my family.

Come to think of it, it was funny how I hadn't seen Lance in a while. After things died down between my uncle and him, I saw him on occasion. I figured every dog had its day. Lance would get what he deserved. I tried warning Chenoa about him when they were messing around. She knew he wasn't faithful or trustworthy. He was a ladies' man.

I thought Lance was straight as far as looks were concerned. Despite everything else, they made a handsome couple. I didn't like Chenoa's passiveness but admired her beauty. Chenoa always had the lead in the beauty department, not because of her bronze complexion caused by the sun giving her skin a permanent passion mark, but because of her full lips. They were the kind of lips white girls, like Angelina Jolie, dreamed of having and were only made possible by making routine visits to the doctor for collagen injections. Chenoa's also had eyes that were dark brown. They were the window to her soul and revealed thoughts I'm sure she wanted kept secret. She kept her hair naturally long, and it streamed down her back. Chenoa also took care of her body. In order to maintain her cute figure, she walked every morning during and after her pregnancy.

Her looks alone weren't the only reason people thought Chenoa was beautiful. Her personality also played a part. She was short in stature, but had a big heart. She would give you the shirt off her back, even if you didn't ask her for it, which was probably why she didn't have much for herself. As for me, I wasn't giving anybody shit that easy, unless that person was real about their hustle and knew how serious I was about mine.

I love my sister but my nephew, Demetri, always had a soft place in my heart. About three years ago, Chenoa announced her pregnancy. She was scared to ask Uncle Charm for money, so I planned a big baby shower for her seven months later. Because of all of the people I'd invited, it was unnecessary for me to buy Chenoa things for the baby. To express my appreciation to her guests, I made arrangements for her shower to be held at one of the nicer banquet halls in the northeast, a place called Chef Joseph's. This place was ideal for weddings, but with my creative touch, using it for a baby shower was even better.

Looking for elegance, I chose the room with a fireplace and waterfall for the actual baby shower to be held. Chenoa knew she was having a boy, so the color schemes were blue and yellow. We surrounded the facility with real ducks because Chenoa had a thing for them. Ducks floated in the pond outside the entry way. I wanted the guests to enjoy them as they walked in. Rubber ducks floated in the air, while hanging from curly ribbons that were attached to the inflated yellow and blue balloons. Baby blankets with a rubber duck pattern were made. They were made big enough to cover all twenty tables with matching seat covers. We even had miniature rubber ducks floating in the punch being served. And of course, the duck cake was specially made and transported from Baltimore, Maryland's finest bakery, Ace of Cakes.

Ordering the food was my biggest challenge. I wanted to accommodate Chenoa's guests by serving dishes suitable to meet any diet. I figured the guests would appreciate the menu if I provided something for everyone to order and enjoy. The chef prepared a choice of chicken cordon bleu, prime rib, broiled rock lobster tail, twice baked potatoes, garden salad, and a mixture of imported breads from Italy to choose from. To match the color scheme, I wore a navy blue Chanel Pantsuit because baby blue just wasn't my color. Chenoa and our mom wore baby blue dresses that were very appropriate for the occasion.

When I took my last look around the room, it looked beautiful. The ambiance needed work, though. I found a CD with nursery rhymes and decided to play it to occupy the uncomfortable silence in the background. While we sat and waited for 130 guests to arrive, not one person showed. It was already four-thirty in the afternoon and the shower was scheduled to begin at three. Even realizing how sometimes black people followed CPT (colored people time), something was wrong. The more we waited the more impatient I became. I called my cousin Paulette to find out if she'd heard anything. When I spoke with her, she said she'd received a phone call around eight that morning. The person she spoke with informed her that the shower had been canceled.

"Who called you?" I asked, totally confused.

Paulette explained the situation to me.

"The people on our entire guests list had been called and told the shower was canceled?" I asked.

She didn't respond.

By then, it was six o'clock. Chenoa, our mother, the coordinator, and I were sitting in an empty room, at an empty table, without any guests. We had all of the food, drinks, and some annoying nursery rhyme music playing in the background. Come to find out later, the coordinator's assistant released the invitation list to a family member who claimed to be helping with transportation.

I still owe Trinity and her trifling mother an ass whooping for calling everybody and messing up Chenoa's shower.

Forget Me Not

Before the game started, Lance lifted Demetri back up to get a solid grip on him. Then, he took my hand as we walked up the steep stairs. I didn't want to sit at the top of the stadium because of my fear of heights, but I didn't want to say anything. After walking the stairs, I realized it wasn't such a good idea wearing pumps and a dress that day after all. I felt really uncomfortable with trying to keep my legs closed. I didn't want anyone sneaking a peek, so I crossed them at the ankles then used Demetri's security blanket to place on my lap.

I scanned the facility for Trinity and Nikki. I couldn't find them anywhere. I did, however, notice several of the guys from the entryway that were trying to holla at me earlier. Their eyes were drifting toward my direction. Lanced was getting ready to explode. His body remained faced forward, but his head turned to find the men trying to intrude on his so-called territory.

We sat in silence. I began wondering why Lance told me the lie about sitting in the skybox. Was he that desperate to get Demetri and me to hang out with him? I definitely felt uncomfortable with the lie. I wanted so much to believe he was being sincere this time.

I didn't want to be Lance's fool again. I was ready to leave. I checked my watch. Two hours had passed since school let out. It was time for Demetri to eat. While the vendors walked back and forth with hotdogs, popcorn, cold drinks and cotton candy, I silently panicked. Surely, Demetri was bothered by his hunger pains and I didn't want him to begin acting out. His sippy cup was empty. I started to worry. I didn't have any money to buy him food. I patiently waited for Lance to offer, but he didn't.

Just as I was getting ready to ask Lance about the skybox, I was interrupted by his cell phone. He received a text message letting him know his room was ready. Lance often lied to me in the past. I felt relieved thinking this could mean he had changed.

When we entered the room, I was impressed with all of the perks. There were two tables with a spread of Buffalo wings, pizza, finger sandwiches, potato wedges, nachos with cheese dip, and a selection of beverages, including beer and wine. A flower arrangement of forget-me-nots sat on the table in a ceramic vase. The room was furnished with a brown leather sofa and loveseat. I was comfortable sitting in the skybox. Having access to it also provided us with the choice of either watching the game through the big glass window facing the basketball court or watching it on the mega-sized plasma television. I chose to watch the game on the plasma television. Challenging my fear of heights by watching the game through the window didn't interest me. My fear was far too great.

After eating, Lance poured me a glass of wine. Because I was underage, I wasn't interested in drinking any of the alcoholic beverages. But, Lance insisted. He wanted me to drink at least a glass so I could relax. I figured it would be okay even though I wasn't much of a drinker. I also figured since Demetri had both of his parents present to look after him, I shouldn't have anything to worry about.

Because of the wine, I must have gotten too relaxed and fell asleep slumped against the couch's armrest. When I opened my eyes, standing five feet over me was a girl with dark chocolate skin, high cheekbones, and a bobbed haircut. She glared at me, while her small lips formed a straight line as she pressed them together. Her lips rapidly trembled, warning that speaking profanities was their only ambition.

"Who the fuck are you and, Lance, why the fuck is she in my skybox!?"

She must have easily walked in. There were only two curtains separating us from the lobby.

"Yo! Wait one fuck'n minute!" Lance said. "First of all, dis is not ya skybox, so letz get dat shit straight right now. You don't come in here talkin to ma baby motha like dat. Yeah, you got me da hook up and I know ya cousin manage dis place, but I paid for dis shit. Since you didn't come in here correct, get da fuck out!"

"Well, I don't understand Lance," the girl said, lowering her voice. "What's up? You didn't tell me you had a baby mother. Where did she come from? What am I suppose to think? I mean, you did ask me to meet you here, right?"

"Yeah bitch, I did, but I don't even like da way you jus went off like dat. So, just get the fuck outta here before I do more than jus give yo ass a tawk'n to!"

After she left the room crying, Lance told me that she was just a friend. He wanted me to know she was just someone he kicked it with every now and then. I felt sorry for the girl. I knew what it was like being blown off or disrespected by someone you cared about. But, I also felt hopeful. I wanted us to become a family. I appreciated how Lance stood up for Demetri and me. For so long, I took care of myself without the help from anyone and, for once, it felt nice knowing Lance wouldn't let anything happen to us. But to be honest, I barely watched the game after the drama. I couldn't get back into relaxed mode.

The game ended, and people started leaving. Before Lance left the room to give his parking ticket to the valet, he asked me to meet him in the front of the building. He did this in advance to avoid the long wait for his car. I didn't want to leave without checking with Trinity and Nikki. I wanted to make sure they knew that Demetri and I were planning to ride home with Lance.

I headed for the elevator because I couldn't stomach walking down the steep stairs. I felt intoxicated and a migraine headache was developing from drinking three glasses of wine. I shouldn't have let Lance talk me into that. I shouldn't have let Lance talk me into lots of things, but I had.

When Demetri and I stepped off the elevator, I was afraid to walk because a crowd of people had gathered around. I could only get the gist of what I thought was going on because my vision was obscured. I saw Nikki from a distance arguing with a small framed girl not much thinner than her. The girl was shorter than Nikki and more attractive. I assumed she must have been Rhonda, the girl Nikki talked about in the car. I could see why Nikki felt threatened. On the other hand, I believed Nikki should have checked her man instead of approaching Rhonda. It takes two to tango. She didn't really know what her man was doing with Rhonda behind her back.

I moved closer. I saw Nikki mush Rhonda in her face. The fight was on. Nikki must have thought she was going to wipe the floor with Rhonda. But instead, Rhonda had the upper hand. I wouldn't have thought someone as petite as Rhonda would be so strong. She lifted Nikki up and then slammed her on her head. Even from a distance, I could hear Nikki's neck crack.

Lying on her back, Nikki's arms swung and her legs kicked, but Rhonda remained in position. Her legs were straddled around Nikki. She took a pair of brass bracelets off her wrists then skillfully positioned them on her knuckles. She continuously pounded Nikki's face with them.

It took several guys to get Rhonda off Nikki. My eyes searched around for Trinity, but as usual, she was nowhere to be found. I tried making my way out of the building, but couldn't because of all of the commotion. I stood motionless with Demetri in my arms. I tried staying clear of any risk of us getting injured. When I heard two gun shots, everyone ran wild. Demetri screamed, his voice melding with the other high pitched screams echoing from the bottom lobby.

Anxiously making my way out of the building, I lost one of my cheap shoes due to all of the trampling. So much for the support from the straps, I thought. The front of my dress tore up the middle, exposing everything I avoided showing earlier. My hair was a mess. My ankle was twisted from trying to run with one high heel shoe and carrying a scared, forty-pound little boy in a state of distress like his mother.

Outside, everyone swiftly ran to their cars and disappeared, desperately afraid of encountering a bullet that didn't have a name. I stood in front of the building hoping to see Trinity or Lance, but instead saw Nikki and Rhonda being shoved into separate police cruisers. I should have known Trinity had disappeared. She was her mother's daughter. I figured she jumped in the car with someone else.

Looking stupid standing at the curb with my son, I rethought my situation. I didn't have much choice but to find Lance. I walked back and stood in front of the building for almost twenty minutes, waiting for him. I tried going back inside to wait, but the doors to the Civic Center were locked. I allowed several police cruisers, and ambulances pass without flagging them. A fire truck stopped. The driver rolled down his window.

"Miss, are you okay?" the fireman asked.

"Yes, I'm okay," I said, while Demetri was still crying.

"Can I get you a ride somewhere? It looks like a storm is coming."

"No, my boyfriend is picking us up. He'll be here soon."

"Are you sure?" he asked again, while glancing up at the sky.

"Yes, I'm sure. Thank you."

"Okay," he shrugged his shoulders and then drove off.

As I continued waiting, the sky became almost pitch dark, setting off a gloomy appearance. The forecast I predicted earlier was becoming a reality. I regretted not accepting the ride the firefighter offered. Lance wasn't going to show. I was stranded again. Looking up at the sky, I decided to call my sister, Deloris. I hoped maybe she would be available to pick up Demetri and me. But, I was hesitant. I contemplated on where the conversation would lead, especially once she found out I was forty-five minutes away from home and had accepted a ride from Trinity and her friend. And I couldn't mention Lance to her whatsoever.

I began thinking that maybe Deloris wouldn't be as upset as I thought. Maybe she would be thrilled hearing how Nikki started a fight, got her ass kicked, and then ended up getting arrested. And she hated Trinity. Even though it wasn't Trinity who received the ass kicking, she would have found pleasure simply knowing it happened to someone she knew.

When I built up the courage to finally call her, I reached in Demetri's diaper bag again for my cell phone and then remembered why I was wasting my time searching for it. I threw the diaper bag down on the ground. The rain poured down on us. I covered my baby's head and tried to shush him. His father forgot about us again.

Deloris
Chapter Four

Too Cool for Comfort

I was exhausted, which totally defeated the purpose of me going to the nail parlor. I thought by going it would have given me the chance to relax and get away from some of the drama. That day, the technician was not on top of her game. She needed to change my polish three times before she actually got it right. I eventually made it home in the rain.

Ronald, a new guy I had been seeing for three months, seemed to have himself together. I wasn't going to be pressured into committing to a relationship though, especially if it required seeing me on a daily basis. Ronald wasn't only fine, but he was exceedingly intelligent. He was a software engineer, employed by the Federal Government. He wasn't nearly as close to being the type of guy I previously dated, but he made good money and carried health insurance. I'm no wiz but I knew a good catch when I saw one. I met him at the mall at Saks, while shopping for the latest Jimmy Choo Shoes that were on display. I know you should never trust a man who likes what he sees, and then bluntly compliments you on how your body entices him. I liked his honesty. He knew what he liked and I knew what I wanted.

When I checked him out from head to toe, I couldn't help but notice his clean-cut, waved hair. I suddenly felt like I needed Dramamine to help rid myself of the sea sickness I got from being swept away in those waves. When I glanced down at his feet, he was wearing the new thousand dollar Dolce and Cabaña Shoes that were featured in Black Male Magazine two weeks prior. I enjoyed flipping through pages and checking out the hotties in the male magazines. Occasionally, I would run across an article or two that would strike my attention. It was seldom when I found an article on a brother opening up and expressing his sensitive side, so when I did, I paid close attention. I think these articles helped me learn how to control my ABWS (Angry Black Woman Syndrome).

In the magazines, ABWS seemed to always be one of the main issues black men had with their so called "black drama queens." I don't think black men were that difficult to figure out. All they wanted was support from their women without all of the judging and nagging that usually came along with it. But quite frankly, that was a two way street. If support was needed, recognizing that the black woman was the backbone of the family should be imperative to the black man. It took strength and courage in order to hold things down. Most of the time, the strength of the black woman was misunderstood, until put into a situation where the unnecessary drama, created by the black man, needed to be dealt with. The black man should understand that behind every good man was a good woman. If they weren't opening up and talking or expressing their needs, how were we supposed to know what was going on in their heads? I guessed they must think black women could read minds, that they were related to Dionne Warrick and her psychic friends.

There was always drama in relationships, which was why I wasn't too anxious to be in one. I had a lot going on in my life, so whenever the opportunity presented itself for me to enjoy a quiet evening at home,

I took full advantage of it. I lived in a four bedroom, raised ranch split-style home with an attached garage. My home was located in the suburbs of Hartford. When entering my home, a Swarovski crystal chandelier captured attention as it hung from the ceiling of the middle of the foyer. The walls were painted egg shell, surrounded by African art. The stairwell led to the kitchen and dining room with an open floor plan. The kitchen countertops and island were marble with earth tone shades to match Italian leather stools and kitchen accessories. All of my appliances were stainless steel. The floor was the color of caramel made of stone. My fully furnished dining room was visible from the kitchen. A smaller version crystal chandelier, similar to the one in foyer, hung over the cherry wood dining table. The floor in the dining and living room were also made of cherry wood. My love seat, couch, and chase lounge furniture were soft suede with a gold and burgundy print. The large bay windows were covered with gold silk and satin drapes with burgundy pull tassels. The living room also had sliding doors that led to the patio overlooking the in ground pool. The bedrooms were all located on the upper level of the house.

I wasn't expecting to hear from Ronald. When he called me, he was standing outside at my front door.

"Deloris, open the door," he shouted.

"Open the door, what happened to calling first?" I asked.

I looked at the phone as if I could read the expression on his face.

"I am calling. Stop playing and open the door," he said.

I heard him lean against the door.

"I'm not opening the door Ronald. I'm busy," I said.

I held the phone closer to my ear.

"So, you're going to let me just stand out here? I told you earlier I wanted to see you."

He sounded pitiful.

"Wanting to see me doesn't mean you can pop up at my house unannounced anytime you feel like it. I thought we discussed this?"

"Okay, my bad. Now, will you open the door? I'm looking like a fool out here."

"Good, you're starting off on the wrong foot with this relationship. Call me tomorrow."

Then I walked away leaving him standing there for a while. I was playing a game and wanted to get my point across.

I walked upstairs to the kitchen and poured a glass of White Zinfandel. I needed something fast to help prohibit my tongue from saying something I probably wouldn't have regretted saying later. Ronald and I had already discussed calling before coming over. He knew I did not like the popping over shit that he continuously did. I had plans that didn't include him.

After relaxing, my plans for the rest of the evening were to drive over to my sister's house, until it started raining cats and dogs outside. Earlier that day, I tried calling her phone. I wanted her to know I was going to be picking Demetri up, but couldn't reach her. I found that very unusual for Chenoa, because she was so much of a homebody. I figured she must have silenced her phone during school hours and forgot to change back to the ringer.

When I finally unlocked the door for Ronald, he timidly pushed the door open and slipped inside. When we got upstairs, he scanned the living room as if he thought I was entertaining someone other than myself. He had the nerve to look frustrated. I think because of the length of time I made him wait outside, as if he was invited over. I knew he was pissed by the way he clinched his upper and lower rear teeth together, which aggravated me because of the sound it made when he did it.

I wanted to give him attitude but was mesmerized by the water droplets dripping down his buffed biceps. He removed his drenched shirt and dropped it onto my freshly waxed cherry wood floor. But I didn't care about the floor anymore. As he walked toward me, his abdominal muscles flexed and stirred the tigress inside of me. He pressed me down onto the sofa. My tongue licked some of the droplets off his chest. His hand swiftly worked its way up my dress and tore off my overpriced panties. I didn't need any more foreplay than that. I reached and unbuckled his belt and then unfastened his pants. The zipper made a slow rumble when my fingers grabbed the clasp and pulled it down. Ronald reached in his pocket and tore open a gold condom wrapper with the word magnum written on it. I watched him roll it on. It fit. I liked that.

He stepped out of his pants and boxer shorts, flipped me over and then prompted me on my knees. I helped him pull my dress over my head. He tossed it on the floor in the direction where his shirt was. I wasn't wearing a bra. I felt the sting after he smacked me on the ass a few times. He placed both hands on my hips and slid me backward in position to meet him. He entered me.

"Damn, you're making me feel really good right now," I breathed, one hand held onto the couch for leverage and the other squeezed his thigh and forced him forward.

"Say it again," he heaved and smacked me on my ass a few more times. I loved it.

"You feel good," I choked out. My legs were shaking. I wanted more.

"What was that shit you were talking earlier?" he growled. "Say that shit, huh!"

His thrusts got faster and harder. I couldn't speak. I moaned uncontrollably. I couldn't remember what I said earlier. All I could think of was giving him a key to my house.

Psycho Path

S tanding outside of the arena, the rain fell so hard it stung, like it was piercing through my skin with every drop. That was my warning to find cover before it got any worse. I wanted to run, but my bare feet were slipping in grass that had turned to muck from all of the water and the cars that were parked there. My ankle was throbbing. I couldn't think about what to do next. But, I knew I needed to do something quick. If I felt the pain from the blows of the rain, I was sure Demetri was in agony. He kept screaming ouch. I looked for shelter. I noticed a red lit sign about one quarter of a block down the street. It read, "Clinic."

Because I could barely walk myself, I put Demetri down on his feet. I made him take one for the team. After setting him down, I picked up his diaper bag from the ground. The bag was soaked and dripping with mud. I started limping to the lit sign, hoping for some dryness and relief for my ankle.

As I approached the double automatic doors, they immediately swung open. There was an older black woman sitting at the front desk.

She was petite and wore a white lab jacket. Her hair was mostly white but visible strands of black seeped through. She wore small narrow glasses that sat on her pudgy nose. She looked over them when she spoke.

"May I help you?" she asked.

"Yes, please. I twisted my ankle."

"Sure, have a seat. I'll be right with you."

Before taking a seat, the woman glanced at Demetri, glanced at me, and then glanced at my ripped dress that was hanging off my bruised shoulder. After opening the linen closet, she pulled two white towels out then handed them to me.

"Is this your first time here?"

"Yes, I just came from the Civic Center."

"How did that happen?" the woman asked, while looking down at my ankle.

"Well, I was running and lost my shoe and guess I must have-"

Another woman wearing a gray skirt suit interrupted me. The suit was so tight-fitted I thought she was going to burst out of it.

"What do we have here?" the lady asked Demetri, but he hid his face; he was as tired and as ready to go home as I was.

"I was just saying how I was running and-"

The woman cut me off, again.

"Why were you running?" She asked, while giving me a suspicious look and then checked out my bruises. I had a black and blue mark on my foot. Someone steeped on it while we were running out of the building. My shoulder on the opposite side of carrying Demetri was also bruised from being slammed into a wall.

I guess from all the frustration of not being allowed to complete my sentences, I looked up with annoyance and noticed a different sign posted on the wall behind her. It read, "Psychiatric Clinic."

"Ma'am, do you have identification?"

My knees began knocking, competing with the pulsation from my throbbing ankle.

"Yes, but I don't think I'm at the right hospital. Can I use your phone to call my sister?"

A lady in the lobby stared, as I tried avoiding the assessment process. I was afraid, especially after reading the words "Social Worker" on the badge laying flat against the woman's gray suit jacket.

I needed to get out of there fast, especially looking the way I did. I figured Demetri would probably save me from getting into trouble. He wasn't harmed in any way and looked well taken care of. He was soaked but continued playing normally without pitching any fits with a toy he pulled out of a box in the lobby.

As I waited for a response to use the phone, I hoped the two women were both willing to help me instead of being spiteful. They were well aware of the situation that occurred at the basketball game. The news was on in the lobby and the incident was being reported. I couldn't figure out the reason for putting me through this unnecessary process. I didn't want to take any chances so I cooperated and gave whatever information they needed. Once I gave the woman behind the desk my name, she looked me up in the system, while a security guard stood over me. He was just as spiteful as they were. He knew I wasn't a crazy person endangering a minor. I looked like I had gotten beat up by my boyfriend or had forgotten to take medication but that wasn't the case.

Demetri and I were in a mess. We were stranded without any money to get home. Not to mention, the smell I probably had from the alcohol I drank. I tried holding it together. I didn't want them to know how irresponsible I was. The last thing I needed from the social worker was for her to snatch Demetri and place him in foster care. When the social worker gave this annoying sigh, I assumed she was ready to interrogate me, but she just gave me a blank look instead. I wasn't going to wait for her to ask questions. I was determined to tell the rest of my story. I looked back at her and then explained what happened.

"I was brought here by my cousin. She was supposed to bring us home after school, but decided to bring us to the basketball game at the Civic Center. I was trying to avoid getting hurt and twisted my ankle while running from the gunshots. My cousin left us here and now I'm trying to get home."

I didn't bother telling her how it was really Lance who left us. Nor did I mention not having any money.

"May I use the telephone to call my sister?" I asked, again, and then explained. "I live forty-five minutes away, so calling a taxi cab will be too expensive."

As I tried getting permission to use the phone, I noticed a woman and a little girl sitting in the waiting area. She seemed very tuned in while I told my story. I figured she was just being nosy like everyone else. While speaking with the social worker, I couldn't help but glance in her direction. She looked like she could have been a model. Her makeup was flawless. She didn't seem to need much, though, because there were no apparent blemishes. I figured she was more mature. She probably wouldn't have let herself get into a situation like the one I was in. She was probably in her late twenties. The little girl with her head tucked underneath her arm looked to be about five years old and kept smiling at Demetri. She had long braided ponytails with burettes on the ends of them that matched her clothes.

I turned my attention back to the receptionist; she was handing me the telephone. She remained attached to her seat. She watched my fingers dial the long-distance number like she was responsible for paying the phone bill. I wanted to get out of there. All I wanted was to use the phone. I would seek care elsewhere for my ankle. When I heard Deloris's voice, I wished it was her instead of her voicemail greeting that I had to explain my story to. I wasn't sure what to say. I knew not to say that I was at a mental hospital with her precious Demetri, being hovered over by a social worker who was trying to see if my story added up.

"Deloris this is Chenoa. Um, I need a ride home. I'll call you back in an hour."

I thought she would be home by then.

I hung up the phone and the woman with the little girl came over to apologize for eavesdropping. She also lived in Hartford. She said she would be glad to give us a ride home, but she was waiting for the rain to die down. The social worker gave me back my ID and walked away once the woman offered her assistance.

I felt uncomfortable. Getting into cars with strangers was what got me in this predicament to begin with. Trinity was my cousin, but I didn't know Nikki. Apparently, the woman's mother worked at the hospital in the dietary unit. She was there bringing her mother's extra set of car keys to her because she locked them in the car. I didn't want to miss this opportunity after passing up the others. My ankle began throbbing again, causing more pain than earlier, so I accepted the offer.

As we talked on the ride home, the woman said her name was NaDariah. She was married and a college graduate, who had attended a university in Atlanta, Georgia. She majored in Arts and Humanities. As a hobby, she wrote poetry.

"Have you ever gone to a poetry reading?" NaDariah asked me.

"Yes, the café I used to work at gave them often. I don't have any experience with writing any poetry but I've heard some before."

"Well, I love me some poetry. I read a lot and watch the news. I base my poetry on politics and things happening in the world. Writing poetry is my way of getting messages through to our people," she told me with a wide smile and wider eyes. "We should get together. Even if you don't recite, at least we can go hang out."

"That would be nice. Where do you usually go?"

"Right now, the club I usually hang out switched from poetry night to amateur night, but I will keep you posted as soon as I hear of anything happening soon."

"Okay."

"Here's my number. Call me tomorrow. We can talk more about it."

I took her number and gave her mine. When we reached the parking lot outside of my apartment, my sister's Jaguar was parked in front. I couldn't see her in it and I didn't think she was until the door swung open and she rushed over to where we were. Demetri wasn't in a car seat. I knew this would make matters worse, so I quickly grabbed him out of the car. I thanked NaDariah and waved bye.

"Chenoa, what is going on!" Deloris fumed. "I've called and called. Where is your phone? Where have you been? Why do you have my nephew out so late? Don't you know it is twelve in the morning? Why do you look like that?"

I was glad she didn't answer her phone, now.

"What the fuck!" she shouted and snatched Demetri from my arms to check him over.

"You know what; you need to be more responsible," she said. "Being out this late riding with strangers, some psycho could have picked you up."

Deloris
Chapter Six

The Hand is Quicker than the Eye

R onald left my house after the rain died down. I felt invigorated as usual. Though he was the ideal man most women probably preferred, I needed more time to define our relationship. I wanted to keep a close eye on him first before making any serious commitments. We'd only been dating three months, so why rush? I didn't feel I knew him well enough and was damn sure he didn't know me. I had a temper that ignited effortlessly. I also had expensive taste and when I wanted something, I operated on a here and now basis.

Ronald and I were so different. I wondered if we even had much in common. One thing I knew for sure, though. We had chemistry. I was like a moth to his flame. If I considered it, being in a serious relationship with him probably wouldn't be so bad after all. I figured I maybe could use someone in my life like Ronald to help keep me grounded. I just didn't know how long I could put up with him. His impulsiveness got on my nerves. I didn't like how he did things like showing up at my house unannounced without calling first. He was working hard trying to get me to change my mind.

Well, it was Friday. I was really excited about having Demetri over. I would have slept in late, but I brought Chenoa to the hospital to have her ankle examined. Thankfully, it was just a sprain. The doctor said it would probably heal in at least a week, as long as she rested. At least she had the weekend to rest while Demetri stayed with me.

After bringing Chenoa to the doctor, all I could think about was finding out what happened. I couldn't wait to get the details. When I received Chenoa's message that night, I looked at the caller ID to return the call, but it read out of the area. Fortunately, she did not block the call. I was able to use *69. When the operator answered, she said I was calling some crazy hospital. I asked to speak with my sister, but the operator tried acting as if she didn't know who my sister was.

Still trying to figure out what happened, my gut feelings was that our fake cousin, Trinity, had something to do with it. When Trinity's mother called mine, she said Chenoa and Trinity were together the whole day. We weren't this big happy family. The red flags went all the way up. What was she doing with Trinity? I couldn't stand her and I hated that we were cousins, especially after she ruined Chenoa's shower.

I worried about Chenoa all the time. I wanted her to get herself together. She was graduating from high school in a few months, so I wanted her to have some idea about what she wanted to do with her life. I offered to watch Demetri during the nights so she could find herself another job. She'd quit her last waitressing job because of childcare issues. It was definitely time for some stability. I wanted her to have funds instead of struggling.

Speaking of stability, I didn't have any issues in that department. I had money of my own. Uncle Charm gave me money regularly, but I didn't need it. I spent some his money and saved all of mine. I never knew when Uncle Charm's generous contributions were going to cease.

As far as I knew, it might happen on a rainy day, so I wasn't going to allow myself to be put in any situation where I needed to depend on anybody.

I was strong and independent. I ran my own business for five years, once I met Brandy, my business associate. We met at a fashion show. I enjoyed attending fashion shows and kept up with the latest trends by attending them. Brandy and I had two things in common. We loved money and shared a fine taste in clothing. But, Brandy had a serious problem. She had a problem that she didn't want any help with—she was a serious klepto. She would steal your drawers off your ass, even if they weren't worth stealing, if you didn't wear your belt tight enough. The only problem with her hustle was she didn't have the innocent look she needed to make her addiction work for her. She didn't have the ability to blend in. Brandy could dress the part but couldn't perform it.

When Brandy worked alone, she managed to get rides to the mall and successfully swipe the items she wanted. When it came time for selling each item, she had difficulty. People don't wear the same size or have the same tastes in clothing. Once I realized how she could make a killing, I jumped on board. There was no way I was going to Niantic Women's Prison for stealing some damn clothes, but I knew how I could be of service without compromising my freedom. I could fence the stuff for her.

At first, I started providing transportation for her back and forth to the mall full-time. I knew the only way I could get busted along with her was by accompanying her inside of the store. If we were pulled over by the authorities after she'd gotten Inside of my car, I would deny it, especially if my face wasn't seen on camera stealing anything. Of course, there was always the possibility of me going down as an accomplice, but I was too smart for that.

After a few months of working together, Brandy began spending more time than necessary in the stores. There were times I would wait for her for two hours or more. I thought she'd gotten caught a few times and considered leaving, but my patience when it came to getting money was beyond belief. Brandy would eventually come out of the stores then tell me that the security sensors slowed her down.

The merchants started putting sensors on the garments. They wanted to reduce theft attempts. Usually, all Brandy needed to do was wear a tight girdle with a loose fitted dress. She would fold the clothes inside of the girdle just right for them to hug her body without revealing any bulkiness. This would allow her to walk back through the stores from the fitting room, appearing as if she wasn't carrying any additional merchandise. That was the easy part. The difficult part was using the wire cutters to crack and detach the sensors from the garments. But it was too noisy to do in the stores without drawing attention to the dressing room. This became a problem for both of us.

Just as security measures became more sophisticated with ink sensors that would spit ink onto the garment when they were tampered with, professional thieves figured out a way to get out of the stores without cracking the sensors. We later concerned ourselves with the detaching process once we got home.

In order to isolate the magnetic tags from the antennas, which activated the magnetic system installed in the stores, lacing bags or shoe boxes with aluminum foil did the trick. Remaining calm, having patience, and being cautious was imperative. Some of the detachers used by thieves to remove the sensors actually had security tags inside of them. They were inserted to alert retail personnel of the magnetic tags being removed.

If a suspect was even caught with any type of detacher, this resulted in immediate incarceration. When I figured out how to remove the ink detectors from the garments after successfully getting them home, I began making the kind of money that was worth all of the aggravation. I wasn't only good at removing all types of detectors, I mastered it.

Business was going well for us at first, but Brandy wasn't moving fast enough for me. She needed her own car. It took her almost a year to make a purchase. But, when she did, I liked it better. She worked on her own time schedule. I was glad I was no longer providing transportation services. I didn't want to be seen in the stores or in the parking lot. I was so money hungry and the more money I made, the hungrier I got.

The pay from removing sensors wasn't enough for me. Depending on how much merchandise crossed my fingers, I made close to three thousand dollars a week. But, I wanted more.

I thought Brandy was good at boosting. I considered her an expert with getting the merchandise out of the stores, but she couldn't return them. Along with removing detectors, I also returned the garments to the stores. Pushing the merchandise on the streets took too much time and aggravation, especially trying to negotiate prices. The purpose of returning the merchandise to the stores was to retrieve a credit slip with the intent of selling it to interested customers. They liked having the option to choose the items from the stores themselves, rather than having to wear stolen garments. Once our customer's pre-purchased the credit slip from us, I used their name to record it on the credit invoice. Identification was only asked by the retailer when customers redeemed the credit slip, so I didn't have any problems with giving names as I saw fit when returning items.

Usually, I received full price for the garments unless the sale prices had already gone into effect, which often happened. Brandy began knowing exactly which items to look for. My Uncle Charm had a connection because he used to date one of the regional managers at the corporate office of the department store. His connection allowed me to access a database, which linked the sister stores together. I began viewing the upcoming sale items, so when it came time for returning, I received full credit for them.

After a couple of years, I began feeling comfortable with my visits to the stores. I worked alone, which gave me peace of mind. If I were caught, I could only point the finger at myself for carelessness. I traveled to the same department stores, but it was necessary to circulate to the nearby states using a broad geographic region. Most of the time, I worked traveling to different states. I thought people would believe if there was a high volume of daily shoppers in stores, that this increased the possibility of distracting retailers and shortening their memory span. I knew for a fact how most individuals did not forget faces. I know I never have. In this business, it was important never to underestimate the recollection ability of someone's memory.

Getting money was my first priority, which was why I couldn't stand having a sister who was so unmotivated. I felt I needed to speak with her about getting her driver's license when I brought Demetri home. It disturbed me because my sister felt she needed to rely on others for rides. As far as I was concerned, she wasn't going to do that anymore. I figured I'd give her my Jag and buy myself something new. It was time for me to get another car. The Jag was probably getting a little hot at the malls anyway.

I didn't know what kind of car I wanted to buy, but it had to be expensive. My profession required fitting the business woman persona. Fitting the persona went along with the job. My closet was occupied with wall-to-wall suits, shoes, and a variety of purses. My small frame fitted a size five dress. I wore a size six and a half shoe, maybe a seven, depending on the make and style. I refrained from getting any tattoos or extensive piercings and kept my hair cut short to maintain a finished look. Because my sister and I had nice, smooth skin, I avoided wearing foundation, but occasionally wore harmless, striking colored lipsticks that glimmered when I communicated effectively.

For me, keeping up a sincere and conservative image was the most important part of my position. Those who knew me knew this was only a disguise, while others who thought they did, needed to proceed with caution.

Chenoa
Chapter Seven

Lesson Learned

My sister kept Demetri for the whole weekend, which was out of the ordinary for her. I was supposed to use the opportunity to relax, but decided to hang out with my new friend, NaDariah. Because left my cell phone in Mr. Smith's classroom, I felt disconnected from the world. When I moved into my studio apartment, I didn't see the logic in setting up a landline. What sense did it make paying two phone bills when I could barely afford to pay for one? I wanted to call NaDariah to see what her plans were for the weekend, so I went next door to borrow my neighbor's phone.

"Hi NaDariah, this is Chenoa," I said. "You gave me a ride home yesterday."

"Hey, yeah I know who you are. What's up? How is your ankle?"

"It's sprained. The doctor said to stay off for a few days, but I'm bored. What are you doing today?"

"I'm taking Tamara to Chuck E. Cheese's. She loves that place. Would you and Demetri like to join us?"

"Oh, I would have loved to, but Demetri is with my sister," I said, hoping she would keep the invite open.

"You can still come. You're more than welcome to," she said. "At least you don't have to worry about chasing him around. You can find a seat and hang out with us."

"Okay."

"So, the lady last night was your sister," NaDariah asked after a lengthy pause.

"Yes, my sister, Deloris."

"She didn't seem too happy. Was everything okay?"

"Yes, she was just worried because she had been trying to reach me, but, as you already know, I didn't have my cell phone."

"Okay, I didn't want to overstep my boundaries. I was a little concerned the way she rushed over to my car. I felt bad leaving you the way I did. I called the number you gave me but it went straight to voice mail. I thought I was calling your house. I figured that was the number to your cell phone that you lost when you didn't pick up."

"I'm sorry about that. That was really nice of you."

"So again, if you're interested in joining us let me know," she invited me, again.

"Are you sure? I really don't want to impose."

"Impose? Don't be silly. When can you be ready?"

"I'm ready now," I said, trying not to sound too desperate.

"Okay, I need to get Tamara ready. I will blow the horn when I'm outside if that's okay?"

"That's fine. See you then."

"Okay, later," she hung up the phone.

I felt relieved at getting out of the house for some fresh air, but began feeling guilty about going to Chuck E. Cheese's, while I watched the other children play. It was very seldom that I got to have a day without Demetri. So, I psyched myself to believe this was really a girl's day out and I wanted to get to know NaDariah better.

"NaDariah, what was college like for you," I asked.

"It was one of the best things I could have done for myself. Some people were in my corner and others despised the idea of becoming educated. The major I chose wasn't highly competitive, but there were still people trying to hold me back."

"What do you mean?"

"My family didn't have much money and I wasn't taking out any loans. When I tried getting a scholarship, I was told that I would fail at accomplishing that. I studied hard and didn't let anyone or anything keep me from going."

"Do you mind if I talk to you about something? Maybe you can help me."

I felt a little awkward asking, but I thought we had a connection.

"I'll try," she said with a warm smile. "Give it to me. Let's hear it."

"Well, I'm sort of having trouble in English. At least I think I am."

"What do you mean, you think?" she asked, while watching Tamara play in the ball pit.

"My English teacher keeps giving me low grades on all of my papers. When I go to the writing center, I'm being told that my writing skills aren't as bad as the teacher is saying. Because English is a subject that is based on mostly opinion, I'm having a hard time getting the teacher to help me and show me what I'm doing wrong."

"Tell me more about your teacher."

"When I went to see him for suggestions on how to improve my grade, he kept making passes at me. I think he wants me to sleep with him for the grade," I said, suddenly feeling embarrassed about my situation and regretting my openness with sharing.

"Girl, that's an easy fix. I'll help you out." She said.

After having such a nice weekend, I hated coming back to school on Monday morning. I wanted to play hooky, but couldn't risk letting my grades slip any further, not if I wanted to get into a good college. Graduation was in a few months. My ankle hurt, but I still dragged myself in. I was ready to leave the moment I arrived, though. The other seniors in my graduating class didn't seem as stressed. They had the luxury of leaving school early because they'd already earned most of the credits, while I was still struggling trying to pass English.

Almost making it through the day, the last hour bell rang. I dreaded heading to Mr. Smith's English class. I was on edge during his lecture on Romeo and Juliet. My stomach turned every time he came near my desk. The look in his eye reminded me of a hungry snake watching a mouse. I didn't have to wonder what he was thinking. His thoughts were written all over his face.

When class was over, I tried not to appear nervous. I wanted to rush out of his class, but instead, I walked up to his desk. I needed to get my cell phone back.

"Mr. Smith, did I leave my cell phone here Friday?" I asked.

"Yes," he answered, with a smirk on his face.

"Okay, good. I thought I lost it," I said, knowing he had it.

He pulled my phone from his pocket, but he didn't offer it to me.

"May I have it please?" I asked. "I can't miss my bus today. So, I'm really in a hurry."

"That depends," he said, looking me up and down. He seemed disappointed because I wasn't dressed up like the last time he saw me.

"You left your phone and I was unable to reach you this weekend which means…" he let the implication linger with a lick of his lips.

I wished he would just give me my phone back.

"Mr. Smith, what exactly do I need to do?" I asked, with my heart racing.

"Well Chenoa, I don't think you'll be able to pull your grade up on your own."

"What do I need to do? I've tried getting help from the writing center."

I knew what he wanted; I just wanted him to say it.

"No, I think you're finished with the writing center. See if you can get a sitter tonight."

"What do I need to do?" I asked again, still waiting for an answer.

"Nothing," he said. "I want to get a better look at you. If you're turning me on wearing clothes, I can only imagine what you'll do to me without them."

"I need to take my clothes off," I asked.

His cologne was starting to burn the hairs in my nose.

"Yeah, that's all I want. Your grade will depend on how much you excite me."

"Well, right now I have a D. Would you maybe accept cash instead? I can pay you."

"No, you're money's not good," he stared at me hard.

"Okay, call me tonight," I said, hoping he would just change his mind.

"Oh don't worry, I will." he said, and then the smirk came back to his face.

Mr. Smith handed me my cell phone and then watched my ass again, as I walked out the room. I no longer felt frustrated, nervous, or anxious this time when I picked up Demetri. In fact, I didn't have to worry about Mr. Smith ever again. I would pass his class with an A grade without taking off any of my clothing. NaDariah let me borrow her tape recorder. She suggested I tape the whole conversation. I did.

Mr. Smith thought twice about calling me after he heard the voice mail I left him of our conversation. Not only did I receive an A in his class, but I no longer attended his class. I left school early just like the other seniors in my class. If Mr. Smith wanted to see something pink so badly, the termination pink slip from administration would be sufficient enough if he messed with me again.

Deloris
Chapter Eight

My Sister's Keeper

When I brought Demetri home, I felt it was worth having a conversation with Chenoa.

"Chenoa, I think it's time for you to start making some moves," I told her.

"I'm not stealing anything with you, Deloris," she said, while looking at the new clothes Demetri was wearing.

"I'm not talking about stealing shit. I'm talking about getting a driver's license and a car. And besides, I don't steal."

"Yeah, whatever. You know I don't have any money for that."

"Let me help you. I don't like seeing you struggle. Things could get a lot easier for you if you just let me help you," I said, while looking around the apartment.

"I'm not looking for the easy way out Deloris. I will get myself together eventually."

She gathered Demetri's things and started putting them away. I followed her.

"Chenoa, how long will 'eventually' take? You don't have time to waste. Let me pay for driving school for you. I promise I will let you do the rest. You know you have your work cut out for you with applying to colleges and coming up with money to pay for it. I will let you do that part without interfering."

"I'll think about it," she sighed.

My goal was to have Chenoa driving before her high school graduation. I didn't know when she was going to start applying to colleges. I figured by the time classes began that upcoming fall she would have had her own transportation.

I was proud my sister wanted to attend college. Going to college would provide her with more opportunities for a better future. In order for her plan to work, she needed to eliminate all of the negative energy in her life. She could have begun by leaving Trinity alone, as well as her no-good baby daddy. She didn't have many friends, but she liked NaDariah. She mentioned how they'd spent the day together that following Saturday. I thought she was going to use that opportunity to rest. But instead, she insisted on getting out of the house. In my opinion, after that stunt she pulled a few nights prior, she should have stayed at home. On the other hand, I tried looking at things from a different perspective. If NaDariah could possibly be a positive influence on Chenoa, I was all for them hanging out. NaDariah was supposed to be college educated. I figured maybe she could help Chenoa get into college. I assumed she had some experience with the enrollment process.

Monday morning snuck up on me. I dreaded waking up early. Brandy came by and brought eight dresses that needed censors removed.

"Sorry for waking you so early. I need these dresses done," Brandi said.

"You know I don't have any problems with waking up to get money. Let me get myself together. When I'm done, I'll make a few runs and call you when I get back with the slips."

"How long do you think it's going to take?" she asked, while pulling the dresses out of a bag.

"As long as it takes. How many times do I have to tell you doing this shit take skills? Been have messed around and fucked all of these damn dresses up! Then what? Then you'll be saying I owe you money and shit! I'll call you when I'm done," I snapped at her.

"Damn Deloris, I'm just asking because I need some money."

"I need some money, too. Don't worry about what I'm doing. Find some customers so we can wash the slips I'm going to get."

"Alright later," she said, closing the door on the way out.

I was a little cranky after Brandi left. We had been working together too long. She asked the same questions every time she gave me merchandise to work on. The money was good, but bitch was getting on my nerves. It was time for me to invest my money and start another business. Maybe open up my own liquor store. At least that shit would be legal.

I thought about Ronald and the possibility of settling down. I knew if I even considered being in a committed relationship with him, staying in that business was not an option. I didn't want to jeopardize his job. He said his job paid him a six-figure salary, but that didn't mean much to me if he couldn't manage his finances. It's not how much you make; it's what you can make happen with it. I needed to talk to him so I would be sure about my decision with settling down. I didn't want to be with someone who didn't have their shit together. The worst thing was being with a man with raggedy credit and unpaid bills. I needed to make sure he was financially strong enough to handle things on his own. There was always the chance of me getting busted. If that were to happen while being in a relationship with him, the Federal Government would make his life miserable. I could only picture Ronald working for the Feds, while his girlfriend served time. It was important for me to keep my "professional" life separate from our personal relationship and make some business changes.

For months, I worked really hard keeping matters separate. Ronald thought I worked for a cosmetic distribution company. I told him I delivered cosmetics to department stores. I thought it was a good idea because it was a logical explanation for wearing expensive business attire and traveling to different malls around the region.

Ronald hated not being able to reach me during the day because of my tight schedule. He became so frustrated and wanted to spend more time with me so badly, he invited me to go on vacation with him. He wanted to travel to Hawaii. I actually wanted to go. I loved the thought of taking a little vacation, but had already promised Chenoa I would babysit for her during the evenings. I gave her a few weeks to find a job before making a decision. I couldn't make any plans anyway, not until Uncle Charm put spending money in my pocket. He had gone out of town himself. My goal was to get disposable cash for my trip and have a new Porsche parked in my driveway soon after he returned.

As I continued working on the dresses, Chenoa called me from school, saying she needed a ride home. I guess she must have missed her bus again. I wondered what could have been holding her up that was so important that kept making her miss her bus. When I arrived at the school, she was standing out front with Demetri. She looked so content standing out there even though she missed her bus. I wondered why. Missing the bus and standing out in the hot sun would have pissed me off. I guess she felt relieved knowing she had a dependable ride this time.

When Chenoa and Demetri saw me parked outside of the school, I got out of the car to greet them.

"Hey Demetri, come give your auntie a kiss!"

I felt good because he recognized me. He ran towards me after his mother let go of his hand. As his little arms reached up for me to lift him up, I couldn't wait to inhale his baby scent that most babies lost after a year old that he still had. When I finally picked him up, I puckered my lips and gave his overheated pudgy cheeks a big kiss. After receiving my kiss, I put him in his new car seat that I rushed to Babies "R" Us to purchase earlier that day. I couldn't help but think of Demetri possibly getting hurt from riding in the car without a safety seat. I was relieved knowing I was responsible enough to think of him.

After I put Demetri in his car seat, Chenoa got in on the passenger side. She seemed anxious when she spotted a silver BMW745i pulling up to the curb in front of me. By the look on her face, I assumed she knew the driver, but regretted it. I sensed she thought some shit was going to go down. Then, Trinity walked out of the school building. What a coincidence this was. This was the perfect opportunity for me to get the scoop on what happened with Chenoa that night. As Trinity approached her friend's vehicle, I was fascinated how fast my window rolled down, once I pressed my pointer finger on the automatic gadget.

I stuck my head out of the window and yelled.

"Hey Trinity, can you come here for minute?"

"Who dat?" Trinity shouted.

Bitch knew exactly who was calling for her.

"It's Deloris. Come here for a minute."

Chenoa pretended like her attention was focused on Demetri.

"Oh, hey Deloris," Trinity yelled and tried to act surprised, but I saw past her game.

"Trinity, you gave Chenoa a ride last week from school?"

Trinity's eyes flitted to Demetri and then to Chenoa.

"Yeah, we tried gettin dem home because Chenoa couldn't do it ha self," Trinity explained with an attitude.

"Who are we?" I asked.

I could see the driver's irritated face through the mirror of the BMW.

"Me and my friend Nikki," Trinity answered.

"Well, evidently you didn't try hard enough. I see yo ass made it home in one piece while my sister came home injured. Look Trinity, don't be offering fuckin rides to people if you gonna leave them stranded somewhere in West Hell. I don't know why the fuck you trying to be all nice and shit anyway. You know we can't stand ya ass."

Chenoa was pleading with her eyes for me to stop, while pretending to soothe Demetri.

"First of all, I didn't leave Chenoa in West Hell," Trinity said, while her head danced with every word.

"Yes, the fuck you did," I said, stepping out of my car.

"No, I didn't," Trinity shot back even louder than before, desperately hoping the BMW driver would intervene.

"Yes, the fuck, you did."

Before I knew it, I was in Trinity's face. I hoped her friend would get out of her car, too. I wanted to check both of these bitches.

"You need to be asking your sister questions," Trinity said. "Ask her why she was dumb enough to let Lance dis her ass by leaving her at the game."

I waited for Chenoa's gullible ass to respond.

"Lance didn't leave me at the game, and Deloris don't be starting trouble with Demetri around. Let's just go," Chenoa pleaded.

"Nah, I wanna know what happened since everybody here, Chenoa. You weren't worrying about Demetri last week."

I was even more pissed off because I knew she was taking up for that no good ass bastard, Lance.

A security guard approached us with a walkie-talkie in his hand. Usually after the late bell, he left the school grounds.

"Ladies, please be aware that this is private property. School hours are over. I'm going to have to ask you to vacate the premises or I'm gonna have to call the police."

Shit, I wasn't afraid of going to jail for beating this bitch's ass, but there's still money to be made. I'd see Trinity again. I wanted to pay her what I owed, but I got back in my car, infuriated. I flipped the razor blade from my cheek back to underneath my tongue. I always kept it hidden in a safe place in case I had to carve my name in a bitch.

Chenoa
Chapter Nine

Control Freak

I loved my sister, but she could be overbearing. On the way home, she interrogated me about what Trinity had said.

"How did Lance dis you at the game?" Deloris asked.

"I don't know what Trinity is talking about," I answered.

"I think you do. Why would she say Lance left you if he didn't?"

"Look," I was annoyed. "I don't have to explain anything to you. I can't believe you were getting ready to fight Trinity."

"Don't change the subject, Chenoa. I know you somehow hooked up with Lance and Trinity had something to do with it. You're going to get enough for hanging with her. I can't believe you're giving her the time of day after what she and her mother did to you."

"She's still family."

"She's not my damn family!"

We rode the rest of the ride home in silence. I didn't know where Deloris got off thinking she was my keeper. I appreciated her helping me with Demetri, but she was taking things too far. I certainly didn't like how she treated Trinity, either. Trinity was trifling, but Deloris treated her worst than she would a complete stranger. I put my baby shower behind me. Deloris couldn't let it go. If Deloris had her way, she would have disassociated Trinity and her mother from our family a long time ago. The fact we were blood-related didn't mean anything to her. But, our mothers were sisters and there wasn't anything neither Deloris nor Trinity could do to change that.

Family was important. I also valued the new friendship I had with NaDariah. When she called me Tuesday morning, she shared the news that she and her husband were expecting another child. She was two-months pregnant and hoping to have a baby boy. She said she would tell me the rest on the way to the DMV. When I decided to get my license, I asked her to give me a ride to pick up a driver's permit. I needed one in order to attend driving school, so she had plenty of time to fill me in later when she picked me up.

Because NaDariah had her own responsibilities, I hated asking her for rides, or asking anybody for that matter. But, I figured she understood what I was going through. Even though she was married, she struggled too with taking care of her daughter without her husband around to help. She said her husband worked as a construction worker in the D.C. area. And he had a complicated work schedule that demanded his attention. He only came home one weekend a month. When she told me he worked out of state, I wondered if moving to D.C. was a possibility for her. At least she would get the help she needed with raising their children. But then again, who was I to talk? I definitely couldn't give any advice on relationships, because I didn't have one of my own. But I knew one thing for sure. It was hard raising a child without the father around. Maybe it was easier for NaDariah because she had financial support. She was a stay-at-home mom, so she was able to give her daughter all of her attention.

After thinking about the advice I wanted to give NaDariah, the question Trinity asked Deloris came to mind. Trinity was right. Lance dissed me at the game by leaving us stranded. The same way Lance dissed me any other time I needed him. Lance's actions in the past should have been enough for me to know not to trust him that night. I guess I wanted to believe him that time. I should have followed to the female rule of thumb. Whoever you come with, you leave with. What made matters worse was Connecticut was a small state on the East Coast. He could have found us even without looking, that is, if he really wanted to be with us. I wasn't that hard to find.

Ever since the night of the game, I kept feeling sorry for myself. I played that night over and over in my head, wondering if I could have done anything different to prevent Lance from leaving again. I couldn't think of anything, so I figured the best thing for me to do was to do myself a favor by putting more effort into setting goals and accomplishing them, rather than worrying about Lance and his issues. I needed to get my driver's license, finish high school, apply to colleges, and find a descent paying job. I needed to also think about moving.

I hated the thought of moving, but it seemed that every time Deloris bought Demetri a new toy, the walls in my efficiency apartment caved in a few inches, barely allowing me enough space to breathe. We were so cramped. My living situation gave a new name to the word claustrophobic. I needed at least a one bedroom apartment. But for the life of me, I couldn't figure out a way to afford it. This was mainly the reason I liked my efficiency apartment to begin with. It was affordable and I didn't have to worry about buying a whole lot of furniture. Before moving into my efficiency, I purchased a bed that converted into a sofa that I shared with Demetri. I liked the idea that it converted. I wanted to use it as a sofa for when I invited company over, which never happened most of the time. Eventually, Demetri was going to need his own bed to sleep on. Another piece of furniture I bought to fit my small space was a pub table that we occasionally ate on. The majority of the time, I could hardly get Demetri to sit still long enough or even expect him to sit at a table. His highchair took up too much space, so I got rid of it. My efficiency apartment met my budget; it was clean, simple, and all I thought we needed, until we ran out of space.

On the way to the DMV, I continued thinking about my goals, while listening to NaDariah talk about her exciting news. I refrained from giving her advice because I assumed she didn't need any. Just because my life was miserable, didn't mean her stuff wasn't together. I didn't think she realized the magnitude of my drama because as she continued sharing her news, she asked me to be the godmother of her new baby. I found it odd that she asked me. We'd only known each other for a short period of time. I wondered why she didn't ask any of her other friends. I was worried because I knew having a godchild was a big responsibility. I couldn't turn her down though. Mostly because I was flattered that she perceived me as a good friend and mother.

When we arrived at the DMV, I only needed to show identification and take an eye exam to receive my permit. I didn't have to show proof of insurance because I was going to be practicing in the driving school vehicle. I wasn't prepared for anything else, especially the long lines we were forced to stand in. Most of the customers seemed confused when they walked through the entrance doors. The signs were pointed in all different directions. Customers took their chances by standing in the shorter lines, just to be redirected to the longer ones.

I didn't like being in a room with so many hostile people. The tension made me nervous. The customers were agitated and the window clerks looked as if they were ready to go home. The customers stood in line complaining about the long lines and how rude the window clerks were. I agreed that the window clerks needed help with their customer service skills, but I ignored the rude comments and continued waiting because I didn't have any other options.

While standing in line, an older, white couple smiled at me every time I looked back to see if Demetri was giving NaDariah a hard time. Tamara sat quietly. I assumed we were all thinking the same thing, that the window clerks were rude, after one of the window clerks yelled at a customer for walking straight up to her window before standing in line. When the customer embarrassingly walked back to the end of the line, this must have been the green light signal that prompted everyone to talk to each other.

"These lines are too long. I wish there were other ways to renew my license instead of coming here," the man behind me said.

I wanted to ask if he owned a computer or knew how to use the Internet. We were all torturing ourselves but I had no other choice.

"Yeah, the lines are pretty long," I agreed, crossing my arms.

"If I hadn't worked so hard getting these CDL's, I would have let them expire, being I'm not using them anyway," the man explained, his wife nodding in agreement.

"What are CDL's used for?" I asked, somewhat interested in hearing the answer.

"It's a professional driver's license that allows you to drive trucks, limos, school buses, you know, big vehicles. The most difficult test I'd taken in all my life. I've driven tractor-trailer trucks for years, but because of this recession my job was terminated and I hadn't had the luck of finding work in over three years. I'm trying to hold on to all of my licenses in case something comes up."

I was trying to be a good listener, but had so many issues of my own. I really didn't feel like listening to someone else's problem. I just wanted to know what CDL's were used for. Though I did feel sorry, the problem with the economy had lots of people out of work.

"Good luck," I told him.

In the process of turning my body back around, a guy was approaching me with a flyer in his hand. The first things I noticed about him were his bowed legs that I surprisingly found appealing. He was dressed wearing a pair of black, Coogie Jeans, a matching pullover shirt, and a pair of white, G-Nikes. Not anything special, but I liked the non-flashy type guy.

When he noticed he had my attention, he gave me a smile, exposing a set of teeth that were white and perfectly aligned. He had cute, deep dimples. His brown complexion reminded me of the dark, hot chocolate from Starbucks I craved every morning and kept feening for as the day progressed. His bald head was as smooth as a baby's bottom, but his clean-cut goatee reflected maturity.

My heart skipped a beat. I immediately dropped my eyes and turned my body around facing forward. I pretended not to show interest, but was definitely interested. Who was this man, I wondered. And why was he approaching me? He reminded me of someone I saw before. There was something about him that I found sexy, even though he was probably considered an average looking guy. Maybe it was his swagger or the level of confidence he maintained while stepping to me. He was fearless, like if he wanted something badly enough, he would walk into a burning building to get it. He wasn't shy or intimidated, even after I disregarded his approach. Most men would have turned the other way already, but he kept coming.

When he finally made his way to me, I focused my eyes on the flyer he held in his hand. I also checked for a wedding ring. I didn't see one. I let my eyes work their way up to meet his. Once our eyes connected, I realized I was still being held captive in his beautiful dimples.

"How you doing? I'm Sean. I'm passing out a few flyers for my man. He's having a poetry slam at Vibes Night Club in Hartford. You like poetry?" he asked, still smiling.

"Yeah, I like it," I answered.

"Good. Won't you come check it out?"

"Okay, maybe I-"

"What's this, a flyer to poetry night?" NaDariah interrupted and snatched the flyer out of Sean's hand. I figured she must have been watching our every move because before I knew it, she was by my side.

"Yeah, they're having a little something at Vibes," Sean answered, still looking at me.

"Oh, we'll be there. Thanks," she said.

Demetri was whining and reaching for the flyer. I at least wanted to give Sean my name before NaDariah showed up, but couldn't because of the way she butted in. She made it totally impossible. She took over the conversation. I wasn't surprised because I knew poetry was NaDariah's thing. I just couldn't believe she didn't pick up on the physical chemistry we had going between us.

Judging by NaDariah's behavior, my nonchalant attitude was literally just that. I was almost certain that Sean felt the same connection I had. What I found strange about his promoting skills, though, was how he only had one flyer in his hand when he approached me and I didn't notice him giving out any others. Was it even appropriate to hand out flyers at the DMV? I assumed he must have gotten it out of his car to use as an excuse to strike up a conversation with me. I guess I must have played it too cool, because he didn't hang around much longer after seeing that the flyer was secure with NaDariah.

As I watched Sean leave the building, NaDariah read the flyer aloud.

"Poetry Slam at Vibes, Be-ware, Be-clear and Be-there!"

The line began moving faster, I couldn't think about the man I found flattering anymore. I was at the counter. I wasn't interested in attending poetry night because this wasn't an area of town I would be caught dead going to, but would have considered going just to lay my eyes on him again.

Deloris
Chapter Ten

Keepin' It Movin'

Chenoa pushed my last button with trying to protect people who didn't give a shit about her, like Trinity and Lance. I figured I should let her continue doing things they way she wanted, even though I couldn't see why she would want to continue living her life struggling and allowing people to treat her any kind of way. She said she went to the DMV to get her permit for driving school. I was glad about that. I couldn't stand it when she depended on other people. I wanted her to be more independent, like myself. I couldn't wait for anybody to do shit for me. If Uncle Charm fronted on getting my new car, I would have just gotten it myself. It's wasn't like I couldn't pay for it. But because he was Big Willy all my life, I figured why have him stop buying me things now. I didn't depend on him; I just let him continue doing what he was used to.

It was Wednesday morning and, as usual, I was busy trying to make money. When Brandy called, she said she needed a ride to the mall. Normally, I would have told her ass no, but she said the new line of Versace Dresses were on the floors at the department stores. I didn't want to miss out on an opportunity to of getting paid, so I agreed to give her a ride. As much as I didn't want to, I figured I should bring her to get them instead of wasting time trying to find someone else to do it. If everything went according to plan, the dresses were going to be clean and ready to return back to the store tomorrow.

When I got off the phone with Brandy, I began lacing the boxes with aluminum foil. This wasn't my responsibility, but we needed to move fast. I didn't have time to play around. I began noticing that I was the only one racing against time. I wanted to be at the mall while the employees were on their lunch break.

Earlier that morning, Ronald talked about coming over, but I didn't have the time to spend with him. When we defined our relationship, showing up at my house unannounced became a regular thing for him. He must have assumed because I was officially his girlfriend that he possessed a season's pass to come over whenever he felt the need to see me. My patience with his behavior was growing thin. I hated the thought of him catching me on a bad day, like this day, when I couldn't be bothered.

It was almost two o'clock when we finally made it to the mall. That was a bad thing for us because most of the employees had already returned from lunch, which meant more eyes would be on Brandy. I was wearing a sweat suit with sneakers. I was used to seeing her wear long dresses. She was tall, so she thought it was becoming because of her height. Her hair was tied up in a bun. Most of the time, she wore a wrap. It was easier for her to maintain than any other hair style. She seemed anxious. I didn't like that. Before she got out of the car, we agreed on a time limit. She also agreed that if she couldn't get the dresses to leave them right where she found them. The last thing I needed was her getting busted on my watch.

After Brandy got out of the car, I circled the parking lot for a few minutes to check out my surroundings. When I felt comfortable, I tried parking as far from the door as possible to avoid the parking lot cams. While I sat waiting, I thought about maybe going out clubbing that weekend just to kick back a little. I couldn't think of the last time I'd been out. It didn't make sense having wall-to-wall gear with tags just to watch them go out of style. Going out of style was the only concern I had with my gear. I didn't worry about fitting into my clothes; I kept my body looking tight.

Two hours had already passed, while I waited in the parking lot with the car running. Brandy agreed one hour was the limit. I wanted to leave her ass. I figured something must have happened. I grabbed my cell phone and began dialing her number, but opted not to in case she was in the fitting room. I didn't want to draw attention to her.

Still waiting, it was hot as hell outside. I couldn't run the AC much longer because the gas gauge was close to empty. It was either sweat or run out of gas. I thought about leaving to get gas and a cold drink, but I knew that wouldn't be a good idea, so I decided to turn the car off to save gas, sweat, and wait even longer.

After sitting there for three hours, I was actually more worried than mad. Where the fuck was she and why didn't she just leave those fucking dresses like I told her, instead of playing around in that damn store? Just as I was about leave, Brandy came trotting out of the store with this stupid ass grin on her face. When she got inside of the car, I took a deep breath before turning my head to look at her.

"What the fuck happened?" I asked.

Oh, I knew what happened. Her pupils were dilated. She was as high as a kite. I wanted to give her the beat down of her life, but getting out of that parking lot was my main priority. When I turned the ignition, the gas gauge was on empty.

Before pulling out, I glared at Brandy. I should have kicked her out of my car, but that would have defeated the purpose of trying to make it out of the parking lot. We were both going to be stranded together if I didn't get to a service station quick. Besides, fighting with her in the parking lot would have been a bad idea with stolen goods in my possession. She managed to swipe a few suits. I was still parked in the lot. I wanted to pull out of my space but cars kept driving down the aisle. When I thought the coast was clear, I checked again. I looked over my shoulder to check oncoming traffic, slowly passing by was a security cruiser with the driver inside looking me dead in the face. I smiled back and left him in my rearview.

Chenoa
Chapter Eleven

Snappin' and Clappin'

NaDariah convinced me to write something for spoken word. I didn't want to. I didn't know much about poetry. But after writing something, I actually thought about going up and reciting. I was unsure what I was going to do. I thought if I felt confident enough when the time presented itself later that night that I would give it a try. I figured I would do okay, so long as I didn't let my nerves take over. I didn't have the experience NaDariah had. If given the chance to recite, I hoped the audience would like my poem. I didn't want to make a fool of myself. NaDariah didn't have anything to worry about. She mentioned her poetry involving politics and educating our people. I was concerned because she also mentioned how tactless she could be with getting her point across.

Politics should be about allowing others the freedom of choice and expression, as long as it's being done in an orderly and civilized fashion. The problem with being civilized was individuals had difficulty with allowing freedom of choice and expression without passing judgment, so topics became too controversial, which potentially led to violence.

We were going to be at the wrong place to even think about creating any unnecessary drama. I wasn't interested in getting involved in any political debates.

A few days before officially committing to attend Poetry Night, I asked my sister if she would watch Demetri for me. She refused because she was feeling a bit stressed herself and needed a break, too. But once she found out we were going to Poetry Night, she made arrangements for our mom to watch Demetri and then invited herself. I was still trying to figure out why. She never showed any interest in poetry before. I assumed she had her own agenda for coming. I had mine. I surely prayed Deloris wasn't planning on reciting anything. Her sparing me that embarrassment was a prayer I hoped God intended to answer.

The thought of Deloris reciting a poem scared me. At times, her mouth had the tendency of using unacceptable language that could put Satan's vocabulary to shame. If she decided to speak, I hoped speaking obscenities was not part of her plan. The evening could go either way with her. I expected her to either show her classy side or behave like she'd never been anywhere before. She was the type that could adapt well to her environment, so I assumed that because we were hanging out in the north end of Hartford that showing any class would probably be out the question. I prayed otherwise. My sister Deloris could be off the chain.

Hartford was the state capital of Connecticut. The city was divided into four sections. The west side was where most doctor and law offices and their homes were located. There were also a few prestigious colleges located on that side of the city. I applied at some but I didn't think my grades were strong enough to get accepted to any of them. This part of Hartford was quiet and you would find upper class people jogging and walking their dogs with pooper scoopers in their hands. The east side was separated from the west, north and south by the Connecticut River. This area had mostly water with limited activity. The south end was similar to the north end. This part of the city never slept. It was a high crime area. Growing up, my uncle charm warned me of this area.

There were housing projects, gang violence, drug activity, prostitution, and other activity that made even the cops hesitate when responding to calls from this area. The difference between the south end and north end of Hartford was the south end was mostly populated with Hispanics instead of Blacks. I took Spanish at my school, so I could relate to the culture and language. And, living amongst all of the confusion were working class citizens. They strove to maintain their homes and keep their community positively intact.

Before leaving the house, I made the decision to ride to the club with NaDariah. Deloris was running late and I didn't want to miss out on any fun in case she decided to change her mind about coming. She asked if we would wait for her outside of the club, because she wanted us to walk in together. She didn't want to have to search for us once she got inside. I agreed, but planned to go inside if someone started to harass me. While standing in front of the club, Uncle Charm pulled up driving a Cadillac Escalade. He aged since the last time I saw him. The hair on his face was gray and well trimmed. His dark skin had a few wrinkles, too. He wore glasses that reminded me of sunglasses but I knew they were prescribed because it was already dark out. The wife beater T-shirt he wore exposed his arms. They were still built. One was hanging out of the window.

"Naw! I can't believe dis shit! What chu doing out here, Chenoa? You gone make me kill a motha fucka tonight," he said, looking at me in disbelief.

"Hey Uncle Charm," I said. I thought he was going to try to make me go home.

"Niece, please answer my question. It's hard out here on these streets. What chu doing out here?"

"I'm going to Poetry Night."

"Then go to Poetry Night. Poetry Night is inside. Not out here," he pointed at the club.

"I want to, but I'm waiting for Deloris."

"Waiting for Deloris? Where the hell she at?"

"She said she was coming."

"Naw, you gone have to bring ya ass inside or go home. I ain't havin' dat. Deloris know better. Go inside. Imma wait for her," he said, never even acknowledging NaDariah standing next to me. She wasn't concerned. She was holding conversations with some of the people going inside. I was too scared to introduce Uncle Charm to NaDariah. He made me feel like a child.

While NaDariah and I waited a few seconds for Deloris before walking inside, we scanned the parking lot for her Jaguar. When I saw her step out of a Silver Porsche, I did a double take. She looked absolutely fierce. No other female in town could come close to touching her. I knew my sister was a diva, but damn, this was my first time seeing her in action. She wore a white silk Chanel Dress that draped low in the front, showing enough cleavage to leave room for a man's wild imagination. Her Platinum Chanel Shoes made the heels of her feet arch, displaying her perfectly built calves as she glided across the parking lot. The jewelry she wore confirmed its true authenticity when her diamonds glistened with her every movement. I shouldn't have thought different. NaDariah and I looked at each other, suddenly feeling underdressed. I guess we didn't get the memo because we were dressed wearing jeans, tank tops, and sandals. I had pulled my hair back in its usual ponytail, although I did manage to wear a little makeup.

"Oh, so you finally decided to show up," Uncle Charm asked Deloris.

She was getting her ID from her purse.

"What do you mean? They could have gone inside," she said then looked up at me.

"They were about to. I wasn't going to let them stand out here waiting for you. I'm sorry, what's your friend's name?" Uncle Charm asked, looking at NaDariah.

NaDariah extended her hand to Uncle Charm in the car.

"I'm NaDariah. Pleased to meet you," she said, as Uncle Charm softly grasped her hand.

"My pleasure."

NaDariah then turned to Deloris.

"Oh, Deloris, this is my friend NaDariah. NaDariah this is my sister, Deloris," I said.

Both of them nodded to acknowledge each other, but there was nothing more than that.

"I see you liking ya new whip," Uncle Charm said to Deloris. He was looking at it from a distance.

"Yeah, thanks again. I love it," she said. Her eyes followed his.

"I think we should go inside," NaDariah said. "I want to find a seat."

"A'ight, catch y'all later," Uncle Charm said and motioned for his driver to go.

As we walked inside, some of the people were looking at us. They were probably trying to figure out if we came together. Deloris had already separated from us. NaDariah and I searched for a table. The atmosphere was laid back with Musiq Soulchild's song, "Millionaire," playing in the background. The lights were dim but the white candles inside of the glass holders on each individual table gave off a warm glow.

I couldn't get in the door fast enough before looking for Sean, the bow-legged guy I met at the DMV. After that day, I couldn't stop thinking about him. I was concerned about his age because he seemed more mature than any guy I'd ever shown interest in. I wondered if he had a girlfriend or maybe even a wife. I looked for a ring on his finger when we met, but I didn't notice him wearing one. I wanted to see his smile again. I loved his beautiful dimples. I wondered where he was. I also wondered if fate did not give me the opportunity to lay eyes on him when or where our next encounter would take place. I had this weird nervous feeling in the pit of my stomach. I desperately wanted to learn more about him. I was determined to find out, though my plan did not involve him knowing that an inquiring mind wanted to know.

As I sat wishing Sean would appear, I noticed Deloris talking with two of the most eligible bachelors in Hartford, Mike Charles and Broadway Fatal, better known as, "The Paperboyz."

Everyone in the room knew how popular these guys were. They were one of the hottest local groups in Connecticut. I was surprised to see them at Vibes Night Club because they had a spot on the south end of Hartford called Cloud 9. Though both men were fine looking, Deloris mostly held a conversation with Broadway Fatal, the rapper of the group. I figured he was more her flavor. I guess she could smell the money on him because she wouldn't have been caught dead talking to no broke ass brotha without any potential to succeed. I heard how they dropped a few albums, made videos, and were touring the world. Their latest hit was called, "Bad Girl," which fit Deloris perfectly.

Deloris sat with The Paperboyz for a while until the show opened. When she got up, more groupies sat down to join them. NaDariah put our names on the list, while I was still scanning the room for Sean. I hoped our names weren't at the top of the roster. I needed to get a feel of what to expect from the crowd first. As I continued looking for Sean, I noticed how mostly everyone in the room was dressed wearing dark colors. Some were even wearing shades. Deloris was definitely an odd ball wearing white, but I don't think she even cared to notice. I was a wreck and was picking up on everything because my radar was on full effect.

Once the first poet finished and left the stage, I began feeling more nervous just thinking about speaking in public. I didn't want to get on stage and forget everything I wrote. The first poet did such a great job. He didn't seem nervous at all. What the hell was I even doing here? But, the love was strong in the room, so even if I did a bad job, I didn't think getting booed off the stage was a possibility—at least I hoped it wasn't. NaDariah suggested I relax. She helped me write my poem and helped me rehearse it several times. She thought I should have more confidence.

Before we knew it, NaDariah's name was being called. She was so pumped up and ready to go. The audience snapped and clapped while the djembe drummer played. It was evident she was a known poet in Hartford. While we were waiting outside of the club, I heard a few people tell her they anticipated hearing her poem.

"Brother's and Sisters, I'm NaDariah. Hear my words and you might learn a little something tonight."

She pointed out into the audience then started reciting.

I'm gonna tell you the truth
Cause I'm a Nubian Soulja
About the history of our people
That the government never told ya

So gather around and you better listen up
This information is valuable
When you're feeling down on your luck

We come from royalty
Considered the first race
What happened to our homeland
We're scattered all over the place

From the beginning of time
Shiesty shit has gone down
So let's talk about our so called leaders
That intended to screw black people around

Listen up Listen up
The info I give you, you won't find in books
The truth has been hidden
I don't care how deep you look

I listened up, I listened up
I didn't learn this stuff in college
My elders built me strong
Come challenge my intellect and knowledge

George was a slave owner
And helped tear our people apart
Developed a conscious later
But couldn't take back the seed he planted from the start

Abe abolished slavery
Thought his work was done
Gave the black people freedom
After teaching our men how to shoot a gun

To represent liberty they built a statue with a peaceful stance
I bet y'all didn't know
They left the original black goddess in France

I guess we should be grateful Abe helped and devoted some time
The government barely gave honor
His face not even worth a damn dime

Listen up! Listen up!

Cause they don't want y'all to hear
I'm gonna push the forward button
And speak very loud and clear

The Tea Party hates us
And don't want racism to go
If we stop calling our own selves Nigga

Then as a people we'll grow

Stop all of the violence and negative activity
We're in office now, let's show some prosperity

Always want to blame the white man
Get up let's get to work
You ain't gettin' nothing for free
You gotta earn every perk

Listen up! Listen up!

Don't self destruct
Then say you weren't warned
I'm here to remind you
And keep you informed

Educate yourself; see I already know
Some of us can't go to college
Cause Bush messed up the dough

The U.S. is broke
Now wanna give Barack a holla
So they can blame him for the mishap
And make him search for the missing dolla

The story I'm tellin'
Is getting older and older
Give the problems to the black man to fix
So he can carry the burden of the world on one shoulder

You better start listening!

"We heard ya," a man in the audience said.

Mostly everyone cheered. Some snapped and clapped. Others tried keeping NaDariah on the stage. They shouted for her to deliver another one, but NaDariah thanked everyone and then walked off the stage with a smile.

I loved NaDariah's poem. Her poetry was indeed about politics. I liked how she incorporated some African American history. I was mostly impressed with the fact that she didn't create any drama and kept her cool.

Meanwhile, my top lip and arm pits were sweating like someone had cranked up the thermostat in the room, even though I felt cold. As NaDariah closed, I scanned the room again, but not to look for Sean. I wanted to get a feel for the crowd. But, I spotted him leaning against the wall. He was staring directly at me with that confident smile that I wished would help the anxiety I was feeling go away. I wondered if it was too late to erase my name from the roster because my confidence level wasn't where I needed it to be. When my name was called, NaDariah yelled, "Do your thing, Chenoa!"

The crowd did their usual snapping and clapping. When I looked at the host, he reassuringly put his hand on my back and whispered for me to take my time. Sean moved closer to the stage then and leaned back against the near wall. Deloris took a sip from her drink then looked up at me. I adjusted the mic. NaDariah was taller than I realized.

"Good evening everyone, my name is Chenoa. The title of my poem is, 'Ghetto Chick.'"

I took in a deep breath and tried to control my voice. I didn't want it to sound shaky or nervous. I held my posture straight, folded my hands at my waist, remembered to breath and keep my chin up like I practiced, and recited strong.

So you say you're a ghetto chick?
No money, no house, no ride, no spouse
Got mouths to feed but continue to breed

Fellas sayin' that's not my seed
And you still won't take heed

So you say you're a ghetto chick?
Like shiny things, like diamond rings
Anything that blings
Will give up that thing
Just to feel the dingaling

So you say you're a ghetto chick?
Wearin' Chanel Shades
Tongue carrying razor blades
Carryin' Louis Vutton Bags
Trying to brag
With titties that sag
Wearin' foot stompin' Pradas
Dolce and Gabbana
Wrist hangin' Movado
And ain't won no freakin' lotto

So you say you're a ghetto chick?
On welfare
Won't comb your child's hair
Neighbors callin' child protection
Phone needs reconnection
And still see no need for correction

So you say you're a ghetto chick?
Mama smoked crack
Stayed laid on her back
Black Pantha Poppa
And he still couldn't stoppa
Come from a broken home

After Katrina had to live in the Superdome
Tried to get a payday loan
Lookin' like you from the Twilight Zone
Ghetto chicks get it together
Instead of wearing leather
Just wear pleather
Cause Chanal don't care when the moneys' gone
And you know fellas just wanna' bone

Ghetto chick you can proceed
Go back to school
Learn how to read
Cause it's never too late to educate
Maybe you can get off Section 8
Invest in real state
And find a suitable mate

When I finished, the crowd loved me! I owed most of the applause to NaDariah. I even noticed Sean snapping. I guess Deloris didn't like my poem because even though she snapped slow and hard. She had a smirk on her face that made me worry. Some of my lyrics conflicted with her lifestyle.

"Give it up for Chenoa y'all. That was good for her first time," said the announcer.

The audience clapped again.

I forgot to ask NaDariah if Deloris was going up, but it was too late. Her name was being called next. I just planted my butt in the seat and took another deep breath.

Without hesitation, Deloris walked up and grabbed the mic. She didn't wait for any snapping or clapping.

"What's up everybody? My name is Deloris and my poem is called 'Digits.'"

Her eyes were focused, looking directly at Broadway Fatal with lust in them. The room grew silent.

I saw you at the mall one day
I checked you out as you walked my way
You gave me that look
As I tried to pretend
That I wasn't interested
Even after my head spin
Armani Suit, smellin' all good
All the skirts noticed
You wanted to talk
And I thought we should
You asked me my name
The digits came next
I gave you my number
But I had a question that was complex
What are your digits?
And I'm not talking about no phone
Cause before we hook up
Your account needs to be full grown
Oooh, that Rolex Watch must have cost you a fortune!
I saw it a mile away
Just tellin' you as a precaution
What are your digits?
Six figures, eight
If so, tell me now
Don't make this pussy wait
Oops, my bad!
Did I say that out loud?
Well if your dick bulges like your pockets
You can make my pussy proud
Those digits, those digits!

Please tell me I need to know?
Cause if it is what I think
You're gettin' this pussy for sho
Don't get it twisted!
I'm not as easy as you think
I'm concerned about your digits
And could buy my own drinks
Oh, you're worried about gold-diggers?
Don't have to worry about me
I'm not diggin for gold
I'm just high maintenance you see
I have issues with my toilet
Cuz diamonds drip when I pee
So what are those digits?
Can you meet me at ten?
If you're not really holdin'
I'll refrain from dissin'
Oh, you like the way my friend looks
And you say you wanna meet her!
Don't wanna deliver the paper?
Then take me to your leader!
If you don't want to spend money
And just lookin' for a close pal
Save that shit for a stupid bitch
Farewell!

After saying her last word, Deloris rolled her eyes at me and then had the nerve to thank the audience. The audience laughed. I was so embarrassed. I didn't want Sean to think I was anything like my sister. I didn't know what to do, so I grabbed my purse off my chair and walked toward the door. Sean followed.

"What's the rush?" he asked.

He was trying to catch up with me in the parking lot. I stopped walking. I didn't have keys to NaDariah's car anyway.

"No rush. I was just ready to leave," I said.

He held his hand out.

"I didn't get your name at the DMV. I'm Sean."

I reached out and shook his hand.

"Chenoa."

"I know. I heard you say it on the mic. I just wanted a formal introduction."

He smiled.

"Your poem was hot. You have mad skills. How long have you been writing?"

I smiled back.

"Tonight's poem was my first. My friend helped me with it."

I didn't want to take all of the credit. If he invited me to another poetry event, I wanted him to know I needed time to write.

"I wanted to come over to where you were sitting but your friend was still reciting her poem. Where your friends at? Why you leave out by yourself?"

He looked back at the club. NaDariah was walking out of the door.

"They're coming," I said and started walking toward the car again.

"I should be asking where ya man," he said and walked with me, waiting for my response.

"My man? No, I'm single."

We made it to NaDariah's car. I leaned against it.

"Single? When I saw you at the Civic Center, you were waiting for your boyfriend to pick you and your son up."

"You saw me at the Civic Center?"

I was puzzled. I didn't remember seeing him there. I looked over at NaDariah. She was talking to someone. She hadn't made it to the parking lot yet.

"Yeah, it was getting ready to rain. I thought you recognized me. I offered you and your son a ride."

His head was cocked to the side. It reminded me of a confused puppy. I was in a bad situation when he saw me that night. I didn't want to talk too much about it.

"A lot went on that night. I'm sorry I didn't recognize you," I said. "Thanks. As you can see, we made it home safe. And, my boyfriend and I broke up that night."

"Too bad for him," He shook his head in disbelieve. "You're too fine."

He looked me up and down.

"I can't believe he let you get away. Well, since you're single, can I get your number?"

He took his cell phone out of his pocket.

"I'm taking the day off tomorrow from work. You wanna go out for lunch or something?"

"Yeah, I guess that would be okay."

I took my phone out of my purse. I gave him my number and recorded his.

"What's up girl? Why you leave out like that?" NaDariah asked.

I didn't realize she'd finished her conversation. She was at her car standing next to us.

"I needed some fresh air," I said. "NaDariah, you remember Sean from the DMV?"

I wanted to remind her that someone else was present. I didn't want her to go off on me for leaving.

"Yeah, I remember Sean. How you doing?" she asked him and looked back at me. "You ready to go? Your sister said not to wait for her."

I didn't respond. I wasn't ready to go. I wanted to spend more time talking with Sean. The disappointed look on my face must have said it all.

"I can bring you home," Sean offered.

"No thanks. Give me a call tomorrow," I said.

Sean nodded. He looked at my number in his phone.

"Okay, cool."

He looked back at me and smiled.

I couldn't keep my eyes off him. I watched him, as he headed back to the club.

NaDariah unlocked the car door. We got inside of the car and drove off. I wanted to hang out longer. I think Sean was disappointed, too. He didn't want the conversation to end either. But, I didn't think it would have been appropriate leaving NaDariah, especially leaving her to hang out with a man that I'd been fantasizing about for the past few weeks.

Deloris
Chapter Twelve

To Each Their Own

I had a great time after the club. Broadway Fatal brought me out to eat to spend time alone without all of his little groupies around gawking at him. He said he actually enjoyed my poem. I think he figured out in order to get with me his game had to be on the bottom with him standing strong on the top of it. After we ate, he invited me to his studio. His plan was to spin records, but I wanted him to spin money instead. I wanted to plan a getaway trip to Fifth Avenue. You know what they say, it ain't trickin' if you got it? Well, I wanted to find the truth in that statement, because I was far from being anybody's trick.

When I got home, Ronald was in his car sitting in the driveway waiting for me. I used the remote to open the garage door then drove my car inside. I left the door up for Ronald to walk in. Once he entered, I closed it.

"Where you been?" he asked.

"I told you I was going out with my sister and her friend."

"Yeah, but you didn't say you would be out this late," he said, tapping the face of his watch. I didn't need him to tell me it was four in the morning.

"I didn't give you a time, Ronald. Why are you here unannounced again?"

I walked up the stairs with him behind me.

"Forget all that. How are we supposed to be working toward building a relationship if you're coming home whenever you feel like it? Can I trust you or what?"

"Can you trust me?"

I stopped climbing and looked back at him.

"The last time I checked, I was grown. Besides, I pay the cost to be the boss. I don't need you questioning me. This is my house. I come and go as I please."

"Deloris, I understand this is your house. If we're going to be together as a couple, you're gonna respect me as your man. It ain't all about coming and going as you please. A woman shouldn't be out this late. It ain't nothin' good in the streets at four in the morning, Deloris. Can I trust you?"

"Can I trust you? You keep showing up at my house unannounced after saying you'll stop. And, like I said Ronald, I'm taking care of myself. I don't need no man tellin' me what to do."

I filled my glass with water. I didn't want a hangover.

"Aight look."

He grabbed my hand and guided me to a seat. He pulled a chair out from the table, turned it to face me and then sat down.

"My job isn't to tell you what to do. I wanna make sure we're not wasting each other's time. No woman of mine is going to be in the streets late nights like this. If your plan is to continue doing this, then we need to part ways now."

He was holding both of my hands and looking into my eyes.

"As far as taking care of yourself, I see you. Would it be better if I took care of you instead?"

He briefly waited for an answer.

"You keep patting yourself on the back. I'm not like any other dude you probably been with, Deloris. I don't have financial problems. If I'm okay, then you're okay. I take care of everything I love, so that isn't an issue here."

I didn't have anything to say to that. Ronald made himself clear. He was financially able to provide if he needed to. Because I didn't like him not giving an explanation for showing up unannounced, I couldn't make any promises for coming home whenever I felt. I was so tired of having this discussion with Ronald; I took my clothes off and went to bed. So did he.

The next morning, Ronald got up and went home. He didn't mention the argument we had the night before. Chenoa had the nerve to call me shortly after he left, trippin' about my behavior at the club. I thought we had a good night, especially after messing around with Brandy at the mall earlier that day before deciding to officially go out. I didn't know what to do about Brandy. Something told me to hire someone to provide transportation for her. I was never surer about anything, as I was about to make business moves that didn't involve her. She was washed up, and I was tired of all of the damn drama.

Brandy's getting high wasn't the only problem I had with her. It was her getting high on the job that caused the issues. You can't mix business with pleasure, especially when other people's lives were at stake. How in the hell did she think she was going to stay out of jail when she simply couldn't keep track of time, not to mention, control the anxiety and paranoia that she couldn't shake with her drug use? Part of this was my fault, too. I wasn't using good judgment either by putting myself in the predicament of relying on a kleptomaniac drug addict.

My day wasn't going too well. Everyone was mad with me. Chenoa was mad because of my so called "bad behavior" at the club. Brandy was mad because I changed my mind and kicked her ass out of my car leaving the mall. And then there was Ronald. What was his fucking problem? He carried a heavy chip on his shoulder when he came over before I returned from the club from hanging out with Fatal. He said he had been calling the house all night looking for me, even after I'd told him I wasn't going to be there. I told his ass I would be hanging out with Chenoa and her friend. What the hell? You see, this was one of the main reasons why I hesitated when it came to getting too involved in any relationship. This motherfucka was acting like going out was a regular thing for me or something. Even if it was, somebody needed to tell his ass that the best thing for him to do was give me some breathing space.

I wanted to change my mind about the whole defining the relationship thing. Ronald had a good job and all, but I was beginning to wonder if putting up with him was all worth it. He could continue his trippin' and showing jealous behavior if he wanted, Broadway Fatal was going to be making more deposits in places other than the bank if he didn't put this behavior to a halt.

Chenoa
Chapter Thirteen

Ripe Fruit

It was Saturday and Demetri was still over at my mother's house. When I called her, she wanted Demetri to spend the day with her. I was surprised. It was unusual for her to keep him for two days. She kept herself busy most of the time. After so many years, she struggled with getting over my father's death. When we were younger, Deloris and I spent most of our time with our Aunt Pooler. My mother didn't have the energy to take care of us. She was too busy crying most days. Sometimes she wouldn't get out of bed. I yearned for the close relationship that most girls had with their mothers. She didn't spend time trying to develop one. I was so young when my dad died. I guess she figured I didn't need the mental health support my sister and her received after the shooting. They saw a counselor once a week until my mother decided to stop going.

The authorities didn't fully investigate the murder. They wrote it off as just some gang-related violence. I can't see how when Deloris's fingerprints were all over the gun. After the incident, my family kept quiet and never spoke of it. I wish I could have been a fly on the wall at my mom's and Deloris's counseling sessions.

I didn't quite understand everything then. I don't remember much of my dad. I only remember hearing him and my mother arguing. My mother complained about him not coming home. Every time this happened, Uncle Charm would appear. He would beat up my dad. For the next few days, things would be fine, until my dad decided to repeat the same behavior again.

I wanted better for myself. I couldn't figure out why my mother stayed in the relationship with my dad. The thought of being with my son's father was nice, but riding the emotional rollercoaster was draining. I wanted stability and the feeling of being content.

I was expecting Sean's call at least before noon if we were having lunch. I was excited about going with him, but was a little uncomfortable with myself. He was already established in his career and financially stable. That was a good thing. It was going to take some time for me to get myself together, though. I kept thinking about a post office ad I saw on a bulletin board in the hallway at school. The post office was accepting applications to take the entrance exam for employment. There were part-time openings and the salary was decent. I thought about taking the test. If I got the job, my financial situation would probably take a one-eighty turn for the best. I couldn't think of any reason why I shouldn't pursue the possibility. I met the age requirement.

I was a little concerned about meeting the age requirement for dating Sean. I was old enough to work at the post office, but wasn't sure if I was old enough to be in a relationship with him. I wondered what his reaction would be once he found out I was eighteen. My first thought was to lie about my age. After giving it some more thought, I asked myself what the point of doing that would be. He couldn't get into trouble for dating me. I was considered an adult.

Sean finally called.

"Good afternoon," he greeted.

"Good afternoon," I replied, holding the cell phone and blushing.

"This is Sean."

"I know," I was so excited I wanted to do a cartwheel.

"I missed you last night. Ya know I wanted to spend more time with you, right?"

"Yeah, but it was late and leaving my friend NaDariah wouldn't have been cool."

"I couldn't get you off my mind," he said. "I wanted to call you last night."

I felt the same way.

"Do you work? What kinds of things do you enjoy doing when you're not taking care of your son?"

"I'm always taking care of my son. It's seldom when I get the chance to hang out. I'm going to be graduating high school in a couple of months, so I'm looking forward to that."

"Damn, high school?" he asked, then paused, wondering if he should proceed. "How old are you?"

"I'm eighteen," I answered truthfully, thinking I had blown it for myself.

"You seem more mature than the average eighteen year old. How old is your son?"

"Demetri is two. How old are you?"

He laughed nervously.

"I'm old."

"How old?"

"Twenty-five," he said with hesitation.

"Yeah, you're right. You are old," I said, and nervously laughed back.

"So what's up Chenoa? Are we still on for today?"

I could barely hear him because of the sirens in the background.

"What's that noise in the background?" I asked.

"Oh, the crew is answering a call. I'm off today, but had to stop by the station for a minute."

"The fire station, right?"

"Yeah, you're right. I'm a fireman," he said, and laughed again. "So, do you still want to chill with an old dude like me?"

"Yeah, what do you have planned?"

"Well, I figure we could go get a bite to eat. What do you have a taste for?"

"I'm a seafood junkie," I said. "I love lobster."

"Cool, I know an all you can eat lobster joint called Nordic Lodge in Rhode Island if you want to take the ride? It's going to take us a couple of hours to get there."

"Okay, that sounds good," I said, figuring the trip would give us more time to talk and get to know each other.

"So, where do you live? I can come get you when you're ready."

I gave Sean my address. He said he would see me soon and I told I would be waiting for him. And then when we hung up. I was glad I told Sean my true age. I didn't want to deal with any potential issues about lying about my age later. When he told me he was twenty-five, I wasn't concerned. I wanted to see what it would be like dating someone more mature than Lance, anyway.

I got dressed and waited for Sean to pick me up. When he pulled up, he was driving a metallic blue, pickup truck. I liked it. It didn't look like the typical pickup truck that most men allowed to get dirty. By the way it shined I figured it must have been waxed a few times that day. The doors had a few silver stripes painted down the sides. When I saw them, I wondered if he raced on occasion, as I only had seen designs like those on race cars. The roof of the truck had a set of five weird looking lights lined up in a row. I imagined he only used them at night. They reminded me of the spot lights found on police cruisers that usually blind drivers when police officers asked for them to step outside of the car with hands held high. I thought the wheels were cool, too. The tires were huge with metal plated rims. The wheels boosted the truck up a few inches off the ground. I needed to use a step bar to get inside.

When Sean closed the passenger side door, I put my seat belt on and inhaled the vanilla scent coming from the tree shaped air freshener that hung from the door knob.

"Are you comfortable enough?" he asked.

"Yes, I'm fine."

I wasn't comfortable at all. I didn't like being in high places. I looked down at the floor for a minute to get myself together.

Before pulling off, Sean reached in the arm rest. He pulled out and flashed an old school, Biggie Smalls CD. He inserted it into the player and selected the song, "One More Chance," featuring Faith Evans. He drove off as the music started playing. The engine rumbled, so he turned the volume up and moved his head to the beat.

"This used to be the hit!" he said and started rhyming along with the artist. He knew every word and was pretty good.

I'd heard the song a few times. I wasn't as familiar with it as he was. I moved along with the beat, too. I wanted to keep my mind off of my fear of heights.

Sean turned the music down a little once we got onto the highway.

"What happened with you and your son's father?" he asked, glancing away from the road to look at me.

"Things just didn't work out. He wanted to do his own thing, so we decided to part ways."

I wasn't ready to answer any questions concerning Lance. I kept bobbing my head to the music. I pretended as if I wanted him to turn the music back up.

"So does he still come around? Do you let him see Lil Man?"

He reached over and gently rubbed his finger through my long ponytail. I guess he didn't want me getting mad at him for being too direct with questions, though he really wanted to know.

"We're not on speaking terms, not even for my son's sake. Maybe later we'll get back on speaking terms, but now isn't a good time for us."

"Damn, I'll hate to find out what dude did to get dismissed. Then again, you should tell me so I can make sure I don't do that shit."

He stopped massaging my ponytail and moved his hand back to the steering wheel.

"I assume you're not in a relationship," I stopped moving my head. "Do you have kids, Lance?"

"Naw, I don't have any yet. I want kids though, ya know? It's about that time."

He rubbed his bald head with one hand and then turned the music back up.

When we arrived at the restaurant, a wooden sign posted on the building read, "Welcome Back." The restaurant had been closed during the winter months and opened back up in spring. Many customers obviously anticipated the restaurant opening up for the season. We drove around the parking lot for a few minutes looking for a parking space. The parking lot was almost full. The only spaces that were left were a good distance from the front door. I was relieved when I found out the restaurant had a taxi service. They had several drivers in golf carts picking up customers.

During the golf cart ride to the front entrance, the outside scenery was inviting. The flowering trees were in bloom. Violets and magnolias hung from them. The air was filled with their sweet scent. We passed by a beautiful lake with swimming ducks. We watched people feed them bread. I loved ducks. I admired their closeness. They care for each other like a family should. I love how the mom duck guided her young and how they had an innate ability to flock together, no matter the circumstance. It was something I always yearned for my family to have. Next to the lake was a gazebo made of stone where people waited until their tables were ready. Sean and I joined them.

When we finally made it inside of the restaurant, I was impressed with the buffet. It included my favorite seafood, lobster. Learning how to eat lobster wasn't a task for me. I had experience because Uncle Charm brought my sister and me to Red Lobster often when we were younger. As for Sean, he wasted most of his on the floor. I tried not paying attention to the other customers looking at us from their tables. I thought they were watching because of the evident age difference between Sean and me, but really they were staring at Sean, who was tossing lobster all over the place.

After dinner, we drove to a nearby Rhode Island beach. We took our shoes off and walked in the sand. There was a difference between dating a boy like Lance and dating a man like Sean. Lance would have never taken me to such a beautiful place. He was always concerned with making himself happy. Just thinking about him made me feel aggravated.

After walking a bit, Sean and I decided to sit on a pier for a while. When I sat next to him, he pulled me closer then put his arm around me. He smelled like lobster but that was a good thing because I loved the smell. We watched the blue waves smack against the shore. They soaked the brown gritty sand and exposed and reburied the sea shells. Seagulls flew over our heads. I stood up and fed them a piece of cheesecake I snuck outside of the restaurant. I couldn't finish eating it and I couldn't see a reason for wasting it.

On the ride home, Sean and I talked more about being in relationships. I liked the idea of taking a long ride with him because we were getting along so well.

"So, why aren't you in a relationship?" I asked.

"I'm always so busy working. It's hard for any female to accept me being away at the station for a long period of time. I sleep at the station more than I do home. My roommate has the house to himself most of the time."

"I can't really see that being a problem. You must take time off? You're with me."

"Yeah, I guess you're right. But leaving my girl alone in a cold bed at night isn't my idea of being in a relationship," he said and watched for my reaction.

"What do you mean?"

"A very important part of a relationship between a man and woman is having that intimacy time," he said and took a deep breath. "Don't get me wrong. I'm not insecure or anything like that. I just wanna know my girl ain't at home lonely in our bed with no one to talk to. Some men don't like hearing their girls talk about the things that are on her mind. I kinda like the pillow talk."

I didn't know what to say because I hadn't experienced pillow talk before.

"Then it's always the concern that I could injure myself or wind up dead working as a firefighter. That could be difficult to deal with. I don't want to put my wife and kids through that."

"I agree. That could be tough. Good luck with finding the right one," I smiled and cut my eyes at him in a flirtatious kind of way.

"I'm lookin' for Mrs. Right," he said, glancing at me from the corner of his eye with a grin. "Not only does she have to be fine. She has to know how to hold the house down until daddy comes home."

"Yeah, okay," I said, then rapidly moved my lips to one side of my mouth and chuckled.

What surprised me about the conversation with Sean was how he didn't feel ashamed with exposing his mushy side. He wanted a wife and children. When he said he was waiting for Mrs. Right, my heart melted because even though we'd just met, I wanted to be her. I wanted to be with him. I didn't think he had a problem with me having a child. I thought he would make a good role model for Demetri being he was a hard worker. He had good morals, too. I liked how he put others before himself. He thought about the disadvantages that a wife and children could face having him for a husband and a father before they even existed.

Sean was the kind of man I wanted. If we were right for each other, my goal was to please him in every way possible. Could I please him? I didn't think I would have any problems pleasing him in a sexual way, but financially, I wasn't ready. After all, Sean had a career. He was probably looking for someone financially stable. I thought maybe if I showed how much I could please him sexually, he'd forget about my lack of stability in the financial department. Would he get tired of the sex? If he was the motivated type like my sister Deloris, he'd eventually want more from me than sex. I knew it would take a while for me to finish college and get where I needed to be financially. I wondered how long he'd wait.

When Sean realized his gas tank was a quarter from being empty, he pulled into a service station to refuel. He got out of the car and swiped his credit card. He put the nozzle in the tank, and locked it so he wouldn't have to hold it. He got back inside of the truck.

"Are you having a good time?" he asked, looking at me then outside of the window to make sure he wasn't endangering us in any way.

"Yes, I'm having a good time."

"Can I get a kiss?" he asked, leaning in closer.

I didn't have to answer. My actions said it all when I leaned in, too.

Sean's lips gently touched mine. His tongue wasn't far behind as it slowly drew a line across my lips. I parted them. His tongue patiently searched around the inside of my mouth and waited for the first dance. My tongue connected and grooved to the rhythm that his tongue orchestrated. My breathing changed pace when his tongue went in deeper for more. My hands held him around his neck, while his hands tenderly rubbed my back. We were in a trance but awakened by a clicking sound.

I pulled back. Sean was disoriented.

"Damn, I forgot where I was for a minute," he said before getting out of the car to remove the nozzle from the gas tank.

He got back in the truck.

"You're something else. I like you," he said with a big grin.

I smiled back.

"I like you, too. I just don't want you thinking I'm easy or anything like that," I said, while maintaining eye contact and easing up on my smile so he would take me seriously.

"Naw, I don't think that about you," his facial expression changed, too.

He looked deeper into my eyes.

"Chenoa, I know you're a lot younger than me. I've probably experienced a few things in life that you haven't, yet. I'm not going to try to rush you into doing anything you're not ready for. I'm not gonna lie. I am very attracted to you. I think you feel the same way about me, too."

He paused and waited for an answer but didn't receive one.

"If we end up kickin' it after tonight, I wanna wait until you finish high school before engaging in any sexual activity. I want you to know that I'm not trying to take advantage of you. Ya know what I mean?"

He paused again.

"In other words, I don't wanna bite the fruit before it ripe."

He smiled.

I playfully rolled my eyes. I appreciated him saying that. I was grateful for possibly finding someone who respected me. But as far as I was concerned, my fruit ripened the day a seven pound little man came out of me.

Deloris
Chapter Fourteen

The G Plan

Two months passed since the first night Fatal and I hung out. I don't consider myself a romantic, but I was beginning to catch feelings for him. He was laid back. He allowed me the space I needed to work my business and come up with a new business plan. I liked that about him. He was also patient, maybe a bit too patient. Before I knew it, I became so busy I couldn't fit any time for him into my schedule. I worked most of my day with Brandy. During the evenings, I looked after my nephew and worked on a financial plan for opening my own liquor store. I visited a few realtors to acquire about buying commercial property. One of them found a building I liked, so I purchased it. I went to the Secretary of State Office to register my store.

"Good Morning, Can I help you," asked a woman sitting behind a desk with a cross and a picture of Jesus on it.

"Good Morning, I would like to fill out the necessary forms for registering a business."

"Sure, what kind of business is it?" she asked, while looking in her drawer through a pile of folders.

"A liquor store business."

"A liquor store business?" she asked, and looked up at me.

"Yes, a liquor business," I repeated. "Is there a problem? Am I at the wrong place?"

"No, but you're going to need to provide me with your liquor license and the lease to the property where your business will be located in order for me to give you the forms," she said, obviously trying to keep the community free of alcohol.

"I'm sorry. Is this a new requirement that I'm unaware of? I only have proof of my business location."

The bitch didn't know she wasn't talking to a dummy. I researched the process to the fullest.

"No, this isn't a new requirement," she said, lying to me with the Devil sitting on her nose.

"May I speak with the individual in charge here then," I asked.

"Miss, I've been working here for a long period of time. I am very knowledgeable and can assure you that the requirements have not changed for registering a liquor store business," she said with a hint of agitation in her voice.

She picked up the phone and called someone to the front. She must have thought I didn't have my shit together.

"May I help you?" a young woman came to the front and asked, looking as if she just graduated high school.

"Hi," I sincerely said with a smile. "I would like to register my liquor store business, and I am being told in order to receive the necessary documents for registration I need to provide a liquor license and proof of my business location."

The young woman looked at the woman sitting behind the desk in suspense then looked back at me.

"The state laws require me, as the owner, to first secure commercial space and my business license before applying for the liquor license. If that wasn't the case, anyone could sell liquor outside of their home or anyplace else for that matter. Here is the deed to my property because I am not a leaser. I own it," I said, handing the deed to her. "I believe your employee is discriminating against me. She told me she was very knowledgeable but I find that difficult to believe."

I looked at the woman sitting behind the desk then back to the supervisor.

"When you give me the registration forms, please provide me with your boss's contact information, too. She shouldn't be working here. I'm sure the state or Federal Government doesn't appreciate their employees using their religious views to decide who to render services to."

I was pissed. I didn't appreciate anyone trying to fuck with my cash flow. I didn't have a problem with freedom of religion or speech. Just don't bring it my way when messing with my businesses or finances. She had the nerve to sit there lying. She told the truth about being knowledgeable about the requirements for registration but she was dumb for lying to me about them. I got her ass fired in the name of Jesus, with the quickness.

I was finally getting my new business together. My relationship with Ronald was getting better. He worked hard with trying not to smother me. I only saw him twice a week. I was cool with that. Fatal not being too pushy and Ronald toning down the unexpected visits made my life a hell of a lot easier. I wanted to juggle both men but made the decision to stick it out with Ronald because I noticed the effort he was putting into trying to make our relationship work.

It was Thursday and my sister's high school graduation was scheduled for six o'clock in the evening. I was excited and ready to celebrate. Ronald and I decided to take the trip to Hawaii after all. We invited Chenoa and her new man, Sean, to vacation with us. We planned to spend ten days in Hawaii. We wanted to celebrate Chenoa's achievement and also hoped to find a little quiet time for ourselves. I was proud of my sister. God only knew how much she'd been through. She kept herself busy with school, worked her new post office job, and took care of Demetri. He was a full-time job all in himself.

A few weeks prior, Chenoa had taken the post office exam. Taking that exam was the best idea she ever came up with. The post office offered her a job because she scored high on the test. I knew my sister had a good head on her shoulders, but she opted against using it more often than she should. I was happy that she took the initiative with finding a job, but I wanted her to only use this opportunity as a stepping stone. I didn't want her getting distracted. She still had lots to think about regarding her future.

The first thing I wanted Chenoa to do was take some of her earnings from the post office and save for college. I was babysitting for free, so she didn't have to worry about covering childcare. Going to college was very important to her. It was important for me, too. I wanted things to work out for her. Taking baby steps and putting essentials needs first made better sense, though. She was finally able to afford some of the things she couldn't before, like buying food and getting herself transportation. All she needed was a crash course on how to save her money without the state getting all up in her business. Once the state found out a sista was working to better herself, they'd cut her ass off and demand all of the money back they gave and then some.

Seeing Chenoa finally getting on her feet made me feel hopeful for her. As for Sean, the new guy Chenoa was dating, he seemed cool, but I thought it was best for her to keep him at arm's length when it came to handling her finances. I understand how finally having great sex could have the ability to leave a sista wide open, but he hadn't even touched her yet. What kind of shit was that? My sister was already the legal age and fending for herself. What was the point with treating her like she was a little girl? I would have the answers if I thought Sean was doing this out of respect for her or just wanted to get to know her better. I thought he might have felt guilty for messing with someone Chenoa's age and needed to ease his conscience. If this was the case, he needed to find someone his own damn age. I didn't know what kind of game he thought he was going to play. After I finished schooling Chenoa, the game was over before it even began.

Chenoa
Chapter Fifteen

Is the Tassel Worth the Hassle?

I was excited. Everything seemed to be going as planned. Sean was in my corner waiting for me to graduate while I stood in his corner ready to live my life with him. Others may have thought by the looks we received that I was too young to engage in a serious relationship with Sean. But, I was ready. A few months had passed since our first date. Things were getting serious between us. Sean and I were spending a lot of time together, especially on his days off from work. We were officially a couple.

Demetri was well. He recently had a birthday. He turned three years old and was growing faster than a weed. The relationship between Sean and him was great. Sean took him on outings to Chuck E Cheese's and let him ride in the fire truck with him on occasion. I was relieved knowing I found a strong role model for him.

Lance was missing in action again. The last time I saw him was the night at the basketball game. I hoped he'd dropped off the face of the

Earth. I didn't want anything else to do with him. He turned his back on his responsibility, not to mention, treating me with disrespect. Sean was different. Sean wasn't in a relationship to use me. He loved me and we looked forward to making each other happy.

I thought about Sean all of the time. I thought about him more often after we decided to bring our relationship to another level. I wanted to give myself to him. I knew he felt the same way, too. When he held me, I could feel his heartbeat pound through his chest. Every time he looked at me, his eyes confirmed his readiness to explore every inch of my body. We planned to vacation together in Hawaii. Then, he would get the chance to do exactly what he and I both wanted.

As I waited with my graduating class in the lobby, I listened for the final cue to enter the auditorium. I slightly opened the door and peeked inside of the auditorium. Sean was having a discussion with an older woman. She was seated in the row in front of him. Her curls were white with a tint of blue and flipped and touched her soldiers when her body turned slightly to hear what Sean was telling her. The side of her face looked familiar. At the time, I couldn't remember where I recognized her. My curiosity triggered a nervous feeling that suddenly upset my stomach. I felt uncomfortable. I needed to visit the ladies room, but knew it was too late to attempt. After giving the mystery woman some thought, I remembered she was my English teacher's wife, Mrs. Smith. Her picture sat on Mr. Smith's desk and was only visible when a student sat at his desk or stood behind it. I experienced both.

Mrs. Smith had a disturbed look on her face while the words left Sean's mouth. I wondered what kind of connection Sean had with her. Was he telling her the secret I asked him to keep to himself? Was he betraying my trust? I didn't know how to feel if that was the case. Sean didn't know about the agreement I had with Mr. Smith. I agreed to keep quiet about Mr. Smith's behavior in exchange for fleeing his class.

I figured I should stop worrying about Sean's conversation with Mrs. Smith. I was a victim. I hated Mr. Smith for trying to take advantage of me. If that meant causing issues with Mr. Smith's marriage, he would have only been getting just a portion of what he deserved. Besides, the tape was in my possession. There wasn't anything anyone could do to delay me from graduating.

As I continued scoping out the rest of my guests, I spotted my best friend NaDariah. She sat with her daughter in the first row that my school sectioned off for guests. My mother sat next to them holding Demetri. When I looked back at NaDariah, I thought how great it felt having my friend there supporting me. I looked forward to supporting her, too. My plan was to give her a baby shower when I returned back from my Hawaiian vacation. When I asked her to write a guests list for her shower, she only wrote ten names. I hoped those individuals were willing to support her on her special day. I wanted everyone to attend. I didn't want the same embarrassment for her that I received from my guests at my shower.

I was also glad to see my mother. She looked relaxed. I think she was proud of my accomplishment. She was becoming a strong adult figure in Demetri's life. I think she wanted to develop a stronger relationship with me, too, and seeing her try was good enough for me. I was willing to put more effort into building our relationship.

Sean was still talking to Mrs. Smith. The front row was full, so my sister Deloris sat in the empty seat next to Sean. She listened to every word Sean uttered from his mouth to Mrs. Smith. After giving some thought, I figured Sean wouldn't have mentioned our secret with Deloris sitting next to him listening.

Some of our teachers were participating in the ceremony. I looked around for Mr. Smith. He was supposed to help lead the graduating class inside of the auditorium with the other teachers. I expected to see him appear in the lobby soon. I became nervous. I turned around to check the lineup. Most of the students were busy socializing or fixing their caps or gowns. I made my move toward the end of the line where I belonged. The departments were divided. The high school students graduating and later pursuing degrees in child development were last in line. I spotted Mr. Smith. He was wearing a black cap and gown with a yellow and red academic hood draped around his neck. He was talking to another teacher and holding a program in his hand. His finger pointed to an area on the program when he talked. When he felt me watching, he looked up at me and placed a smirk on his face that I found familiar. His message came across clear. He didn't feel shame about his previous behavior. I looked away, as Mr. Smith walked toward the front of the line.

After we received the cue to enter the auditorium, we walked in line while the band played the unmistakable graduation song, "Pomp and Circumstance." The girl in front of me stopped several times. Her pace messed up the flow of the procession. She made sure her family took plenty of pictures. Every time she stopped, I bumped into her. The bobby pens fastening my cap to my hair came loose. I tried holding the cap with my hand, but it shifted until it eventually fell to the floor. This delayed the march even more. I took this as a sign that my day was not going to be as perfect as I had hoped.

As we walked, the line moved more smoothly. I took the opportunity and watched my classmates up front find their seats on the stage. The music died down. I noticed the band members looking at me. I was last in line. They were supposed to stop playing once I found my seat. There was a problem. I didn't have a seat. Apparently, my school miscounted the chairs. I didn't know what to do. Being mad as hell wasn't good enough.

"I can't believe this. I don't have a seat," I whispered to the girl who previously walked in front of me.

"Oh my gosh, what are you going to do, Chenoa?" my classmate asked, looking up at me after taking her seat.

"Scoot over. I need to sit with you," I said while ducking so I wouldn't cause attention to myself.

"We're not going to fit," she whispered back still smiling for the cameras.

"Scoot over some," I said again, this time pushing her thigh with both of my hands.

"What are you doing?" she agitatedly asked, and looked around the room for help.

When I forced one of her legs off the chair, I planted half of my butt cheek onto it.

"Ugh, this is some ridiculous shit. We have to sit like this through the whole ceremony?" she asked, while fighting my hips.

"Girl, I'm sorry. I owe you big," I told her, balancing on the chair and smiling with her for the cameras.

"Yeah you do, Chenoa," she said, not taking into consideration that she held up the line earlier.

After sitting for almost an hour listening to the guest speaker, I couldn't resist looking back to see if Sean was still talking to Mrs. Smith. She must have texted Mr. Smith a message because when I turned back around, Mr. Smith was looking at his phone. Apparently, the message he received wasn't a pleasant one. He looked directly at me. Mrs. Smith stormed out of the auditorium.

I still had the urge to use the bathroom, so I was glad when we received our diplomas shortly after the guest speaker. The ceremony finally came to an end. The space in the auditorium limited us from moving around freely, so everyone headed outside of the building. I thanked my classmate for allowing me to share her seat then searched for my family.

On my way outside, I decided to make a detour to the ladies room. I stopped and hugged some former classmates. A few of them questioned me when I headed in a different direction. They wanted to take pictures with me. I promised I would when I finished.

The bathroom was empty. I was relieved I didn't have to wait in line to use it. I fixed my dress underneath my graduation gown then noticed that part of gown had gotten wet from the toilet. I pulled the gown over my head. The ceremony was over so I couldn't see a need to continue wearing it. I walked out of the stall and turned the water on to wash my hands. I smelled Old Spice Cologne. When I looked up, Mr. Smith's reflection was in the mirror looking back at me. I screamed but didn't hear a sound. My voice must have left my body. My heart was still there because I felt it pulsating through my throat. I felt weak. I couldn't breathe. I wanted to run but my feet wouldn't cooperate. I stood in the mirror shaking. I needed to run or turn around to face him. I turned around and looked him in the eye.

"You are a sneaky little bitch," he said, walking closer to me.

His eyes were bloodshot and sweat dripped from his forehead. He was still wearing his cap and gown.

"I thought we had an agreement? You put your boyfriend up to telling my wife about us? I thought we had an agreement?"

He spoke in a sharp but low voice close to my ear.

"I should fuck you now and get it over with since I'm going to lose everything anyway."

When I looked at the door, his eyes followed. I wanted to make a break for it or for someone to at least walk in.

"Bitch, you better not move or make a sound. You will regret it," he warned.

I was too afraid to move or speak.

His body was so close to mine, my back pressed against the sink. My body continued to tremble. One of his hands grabbed my throat. He used the other hand and pulled my dress up. His hand swept the crotch of my panties to one side. His finger scratched my vaginal wall when it entered me. I squirmed.

"This ordeal is just a rumor. If I lose my job or my wife, I'm coming to look for you, bitch! Do you understand?" he asked, with one hand still around my throat and one finger in my vagina.

Tears fell from my eyes when I shook my head. Sean had messed up.

Mr. Smith removed his finger then tasted it. He smirked and walked out of the bathroom.

I wiped my tears and tried gaining my composure. I jumped when NaDariah walked through the bathroom doors with Demetri and her daughter, Tamara.

"Girl, what's taking you so long?" she asked.

"I must have a stomach bug or something. I'm coming out," I said.

Show and Tell

After the ceremony, we headed to my place for food and drinks. Chenoa didn't want a fancy graduation celebration. We only invited our boyfriends, NaDariah, and some family members over to hang out for the evening. I sensed tension between Chenoa and Sean. She wanted to be happy but I could tell something was bothering her. I wanted to change her mood so I pulled her away from her guests for a minute.

"Chenoa, come take a walk with me downstairs," I said, while walking toward the garage.

Chenoa followed, while Sean continued playing in the kitchen with Demetri. When we reached the garage, she saw the Jaguar parked with the keys inside of the envelope taped on the window.

"Deloris, are you giving me your Jag!"

"Yeah, but you can trade it for something else," I said. "I put a few miles on it but it should get you back and forth to work and college."

"This is a very expensive car. How much is the insurance, because my money is very tight?"

"Don't worry about paying the insurance. I'll cover you until you're able to pay without breaking the bank."

"Wow, thanks Deloris," she said.

Because I was in the position to help my sister, I also took the liberty of setting her up in a new crib. Annually in June, the State of Connecticut gathered foreclosed homes and prepared them for auctioning. Two weeks before Chenoa's graduation, I bid on a three bedroom townhouse. It was appraised at two hundred thousand dollars. I purchased it for sixty thousand. This was the amount owed to the bank that went into foreclosure due to unpaid mortgage, taxes and other fees. This was another surprise for Chenoa.

After hanging out for a while at my place, we all took a ride to her new house. I didn't bother furnishing it for her. I thought she would appreciate decorating it herself. Her new place suited her perfectly. It was quaint with enough space to fit average-size furniture. She had a kitchen, a dining and living room, and two full bathrooms. One of the bathrooms was on the main floor. The other was located on the upper level where her and Demetri's rooms were.

Her girlfriend NaDariah seemed pleased. She didn't show any signs of jealousy. I found that interesting. I'd known Chenoa all of her life and had never known for her to have any genuine friends, but NaDariah seemed okay. When we toured the house, Chenoa paid close attention to her. She made sure NaDariah was careful not to trip down the staircase. I walked in front of her, too. I didn't want her losing her baby on my watch.

In the past, Chenoa had a bad track record with managing her finances. At the end of the month, she didn't have two nickels to rub together. This was a good time to talk to her about how to recycle her money, instead of disposing of it.

"Deloris, I am over whelmed with this house," she said. "Did you buy this yourself?"

"Of course I bought it myself. Why would you ask me that?"

"Well, Uncle Charm purchases a lot of expensive things for you. I wanted to make sure it is you I owe my gratitude to."

"Owe gratitude? Girl, you're talking like you ready for college. Your English sounds good to me," I said and gave her a hug. "I'm proud of you little sis. I see you're trying to better yourself. I wanted to lend a helping hand. I know it's difficult for you to accept gifts from me, but I'm going to change my lifestyle. You'll see."

NaDariah joined the rest of the crew downstairs. They were all standing around talking about interior decorating and the different things they would do to the house if it belonged to them.

"Chenoa, walk back up with me. I want to talk to you about something."

When walked back into her bedroom, I was surprised she didn't notice the fire safe bolted down to the floor of the closet during the first walk through. The bedroom was empty and the closets were open.

"What's this for?" she asked and sat on the floor.

"This is a safe. I bought it for you to keep your money orders."

"Money orders?" she asked. "Why would I need money orders?"

"Listen to me," I said, while kneeling down on the floor. "You make six hundred dollars a week, right?"

She looked at me and shook her head yes.

"Let me tell you how to keep your benefits that you receive from the state. They send a welfare check, food stamps, and you have a healthcare plan. There is no way the state is going to let you hold on to all of that with a job."

She just stared at me.

"You need to use the post office to your advantage. Correct me if wrong, but I don't think I am," I said. "The post office accommodates all of their employees by cashing payroll checks for any amount without charging a fee. Cash your paychecks at the post office window when you get paid. After cashing your check, purchase a six hundred dollar money order every week instead of depositing your money in a bank. Because you still need to pay your utilities and have money for everyday things, pay for them with the check the state sends to you every month."

She looked at me with nervous eyes, but kept listening.

"When you purchase the money orders, make them out to yourself. No one else can cash them but you. The money orders are valid up to six months. Make sure you renew them before the expiration date. Are you following me?" I asked.

She shook her head again, and I proceeded.

"Make sure you keep track of the money orders. Find another place to keep the carbon copied receipt in case you lose them. You would have proof of purchase and the post office will have to replace them."

"Deloris, what is the purpose for all of this?" she asked.

"I'm trying to keep you from using a bank or financial institution. You don't want the state all up in your business. You're already in the system. That is not a good thing, Chenoa. You can't shit without them being there to watch you wipe your ass. This way, the state can't track any money that is in your possession."

"We're going to be going on vacation soon. I want to be able to go to the bank and use a debit card if I need money. I can't carry the safe everywhere I go," she said.

"I know. You made a good point. But there are post offices in all of the United States. You can cash your money orders at any post office, Hawaii too."

"I don't know, Deloris. I need to think about this. I don't want to get in trouble," she said while getting up off of the floor.

I stood up, too.

"The only problem I see with this is when you claim your taxes. I will claim Demetri and you for now and sign the deed to the house over to you when you graduate college. Then you can open up you a bank account. You should have a little change to fall back on, until you secure a position in your field."

"I'll think about it," she said.

Chenoa
Chapter Seventeen

Acrophobia

For a graduation gift Sean paid for our trip to Hawaii. I'm sure it costs him a pretty penny. We rode first class and I felt like a princess. I have to admit, bringing me to Hawaii was a nice gesture to prove how strong his feelings for me were. To be completely honest, it didn't take much to make me happy. I enjoyed being with Sean. It didn't matter, as long as we were together. I totally loved this man. I would have done anything for him. My every thought included him, and that concerned me. I'd never felt this way before about anyone, not even Lance.

I wanted to build a strong foundation with Sean. I didn't want any secrets between us. When I told him about the situation with my English grade and Mr. Smith, my intention was to keep the communication open. On our first date, he expressed the importance of communication. I didn't expect him to try and fix my problem. He only made it worse. I thought I was finished with Mr. Smith until the episode at my graduation in the ladies room. After Sean shared my secret, I figured there were some things I should have kept to myself. I wasn't going to let this ruin our relationship or our trip, though. He was only trying to help.

Deloris was due for a vacation. She and her boyfriend, Ronald, sat in the row behind us. I guess she decided against pursuing a relationship with Broadway Fatal. I was glad she found someone to take seriously. Ronald was hard-working, intelligent, and business minded. His good looks and nice physique were all great qualities, too. Broadway Fatal was cool, but my sister needed a lower-keyed lifestyle. Broadway Fatal lived in the spotlight. This was something Deloris didn't need. She said she was going to change. I wondered what she was going to do differently.

When Deloris gave me the graduation gifts, I felt guilty accepting them. I didn't want her believing I was condoning how she made her money. The material things she provided me with weren't important. I preferred having her around. She valued material things without realizing how easily it was to lose them. It was easy to lose everything in the blink of an eye.

As I tried relaxing in my chair, I felt nervous from all of the turbulence. I probably would have felt worse, but we had a good flight attendant. She checked on us periodically.

"How are you doing? Can I get you another pillow?" the flight attendant asked.

"No thank you, I'm fine. I'm just a little nervous."

"Well let me offer you a glass of champagne. This should help you relax some."

"No, thanks," Sean intervened holding his hand up. "We won't be drinking throughout the flight. We appreciate it, though."

"Okay sure," the flight attendant said and then walked over to Deloris and Ronald.

After the flight attendant left us, I wondered if Sean refused the alcohol beverage for me because of my age or he was afraid the alcohol would make my stomach sick. I didn't say anything. I sat back in my chair, put my headphones on, wrapped my arm around his, and continued watching the boring movie that was playing.

Our flight landed in Maui. We were greeted by the most beautiful people I had ever seen. Five hula dancers waited for us with male partners standing next to them. Their eyes were dark brown with long, black, and silky hair. Their skin was the color of the dessert sand. They wore red and yellow tropical dresses with purple and white leis made of orchids that hung from their necks. The smiles from the male dancers were welcoming, almost as mesmerizing as Sean's. As I smiled back, my eyes traveled south. I noticed their beautifully buffed chests and pronounced six packs that were partially covered by leis that matched their partners. Their pants were white and made of linen. The pants legs rippled in the wind.

I thought the airlines must have chosen ten of the most beautiful Hawaiians to greet us, but as we traveled from the airport to our resort, most of the Hawaiian's were beautiful. When we passed the beaches, the blue ocean glistened with silver light. It turned the swaying palm leaves into sparkly emeralds. The exotic birds welcomed us with their striking colors. They flew carelessly from tree to tree, unconcerned about encountering any dangerous species, including humans. The tourists gathered around in little groups. They took pictures of the incredible view and of each other.

Valet attendants took our vehicle once we reached the main entrance of the resort. Sean and Ronald immediately escorted Deloris and me to the bar area located in the courtyard. It was underneath a teepee. The guys left us there and went back inside of the lobby to set up the exertions for the week. We sipped on tropical drinks and watched the hula dancers perform, while unattended children ran back and forth, ruining the presentation.

I needed to relax. I was jetlagged and worried about my little man. NaDariah was kind enough to offer to watch him for the week. I didn't have to worry about Demetri, but checked my cell phone for any missed calls just in case. My cell phone screen was empty but I decided to call her, anyway.

"Hey, NaDariah."

"Hey, have y'all made it there yet?"

"Yeah, we're here. Girl, this place is beautiful. I am so excited. Where's Demetri?"

"He's in the other room playing with Tamara. That boy is having a good time."

"Good, I didn't forget to pack anything, did I?"

"I don't know but whatever you forgot, I will make sure I get it for him. Just go ahead and have a good time."

"I hope he doesn't give you a hard time. If you keep him busy, you should be able to wear him out. Do you have any plans?"

"Girl, I have a lot of stuff planned. I got you. Everything will be on the up and up when you get back."

"Okay, I'll call back tomorrow to check on him," I said, wondering what was going to be on the up and up.

"Alright, bye."

"Bye," I said and hung up.

When Sean returned to the bar area, I finished my fruity drink. I guess he didn't want my stomach getting sick on the plane because he didn't say anything about my alcohol intake while we were at the bar. I felt more relaxed.

"Baby you ready to go up?" he asked.

"Go up where?" I asked, trying not to sound nervous.

"To our room," he said suspiciously. "Aren't you ready to go freshen up? I have a surprise for you."

"A surprise? What kind of surprise?"

"Okay, I guess I'm gonna spoil it," he said. "I booked the penthouse suite for us. It is hot. I can't wait for you see-"

"Sean," I interrupted. "I think that it's great baby that you did that for us, but I am terribly afraid of heights. Ever since I was a little girl, I've been afraid."

"Afraid of heights? There's no need to be afraid. You have me here to protect you," he said and put his arm around me without realizing the severity of my issue. He was very excited about our room. I wish I had mentioned my fear of heights to him sooner. This was one important thing I forgot to tell him about myself.

After my father's death, I became terrified of being in high places. Sitting on the floor in the corner watching my dad bleed from his head was a traumatic experience for me. The closer to the ground I was, the safer I felt because I didn't know if another bullet was going to fly through the air and hit me next. When my uncle came in and found me on the floor, he picked me up high off the ground. Even though I was in his arms, I didn't feel safe. What made matters worse, still in the air, he brought me outside where there were guns pointed at me.

I walked inside the building with Sean. He had already sent our luggage to the room. My insides were turned inside out when we approached the glass elevator.

"Sean, I don't think I can do this," I said, breathing deep and slow, because I was having trouble breathing.

"Yes, you can, Chenoa. Ain't nothing gone happen to you baby, I promise," he said after pushing the button and pulling me closer to him.

I didn't want to spoil the trip or disappoint him. I pretended to be as engaged as he was with the view as the glass elevator lifted us to the top floor. I stood holding him with my eyes buried in his chest. I figured once we were settled in the suite, I would feel better as long as I stayed clear of any lofts or windows. The first thing I noticed was a huge window when we walked in. It took up the whole side of the room and was barely covered by a pair of maroon sheer curtains.

I had to admit, other than my major issue with the window, the room was absolutely gorgeous. I loved the beautiful crystal chandelier that hung from the ceiling. A black velvet sofa and loveseat with accented maroon and black printed pillows sat in the corner next to the powder room. This was my favorite room in the suite. The walls were made of stone and matched his and hers sink bowls made of clay. The Jacuzzi tub was large enough to fit at least six people. Next to the Jacuzzi was an enclosed shower with fresh ferns draped across the top.

When I made my way back to the sitting area, Sean closed the curtains. He wanted me to feel comfortable with his room choice. I sat on the bed and looked at the maroon and black scarves that were wrapped around the wooden columns of the bed. I'd only shared a bed with Lance. The thought of being with Sean suddenly made me nervous.

Deloris
Chapter Eighteen

Diamonds are a Girl's Best Friend

Coming to Hawaii was a well deserved break and hell of an idea. I couldn't wait to get away from all of the drama back home. The first thing I did was take a shower to freshen up from the long plane ride. After Ronald told me he booked a reservation for a luau, I was a little irritated because I just wanted to settle in and relax for the rest of the day. It seemed he put thought into planning a wonderful evening, so I adjusted my attitude. I put on a cute little black dress with silver pumps.

When we arrived at the luau, we were seated for dinner and a presentation. At the table, my sister and Sean reminded me of two little puppy dogs that were in love. They shared the same drink using two straws, like the facility didn't have enough to go around. Surprisingly, the atmosphere was romantic and elegant, though. I didn't think it would be, being this was an outdoor affair. I thought this would be another occasion I overdressed for. I was glad I didn't make a big deal about staying in the room.

The scenery was nice. We sat under a large pavilion that accommodated about fifty tables. Each table was dressed with linen cloths with dimmed lamps sitting on them. I liked the carved handmade wooden vases that held short stemmed exotic flowers. The entertainment area had a raised stage with high beamed lights that could potentially cause blindness if directly looked at. I believe we had the best seats in the house. We were close enough to watch the show without anyone blocking our view, but far enough to avoid any of the performer's sweat popping on us. That would have definitely ruined my evening.

To begin our meal, we were served Taro Rolls. They were purple dinner rolls made with purple colored flour. The rolls looked weird but tasted good. Ripe pineapple spears were put on the table and served as an appetizer. For the main course, we ate Kalua. This was roasted pig seasoned with sea salt and green onions. We also had a Hawaiian starch that looked like sweet potatoes called poi. Mostly everyone drank Mai Tais. We drank them as if they were going out of style. All of the foods were different. The presentation was exquisite and the flavors blended leaving my taste buds at ease.

When the stage blacked out, front and centered stood a Samoan fire dancer. He opened the show. I loved how he used all of his limbs to twirl the fire knife, while the drummers played an upbeat tempo. This caused the audience to sit at the edge of their seats. I even felt a drip of sweat run down the back of my neck when he pretended to let the flamed knife slip out of his hand. All of the dancers from the Polynesian Islands did a wonderful job with representing their culture.

When the show came to an end, the announcer called out and introduced three female Tahitian Hula Dancers. They were beautiful but couldn't hold a torch to me. They wore white and silky grass skirt that hung from their hips. The skirts were held up by belts made of flowers and feathers. They wore head pieces that were spectacularly dressed with matching feathers and flowers similar to the ones on the belts. I wondered if they were really going to dance topless, though. The leis around their necks barely covered their breast. I figured they could have worn any type of bra. At least that would have been appropriate.

After announcing the dancers, the announcer stated he needed audience participation. I was stunned when I heard him call Ronald's name from the audience. My initial thought was there were about five hundred people here, so why was he calling my Ronald? I gave Ronald a dirty look that evidently didn't faze him. He got up from his seat and walked to the stage. Another drip of sweat came running down my neck. People clapped and cheered.

I figured Ronald was the chosen participant for the evening. I remembered watching a show on television when they chose someone out of the audience to help close the show with the finale Tahitian dancers. I wanted to smack the shit out of Sean. He cheered the loudest. Chenoa sat smiling at me hoping I would remain calm and go with the flow. The announcer gave Ronald the microphone when he walked up on stage.

"Come up and dance with me, Deloris?" Ronald said.

I looked at him in disbelief.

"There is no way I'm going up there," I said, looking back at Chenoa and Ronald.

"Come on up, Deloris, and dance with your man," he said again.

"What the hell is Ronald doing?" I asked them.

Chenoa got up and pulled me out of my seat. The audience cheered.

I tried figuring out why Ronald thought he needed me up on stage with him. He didn't want to live in the doghouse while vacationing in Hawaii. He included me in the program to cut down on some of the drama I was going to cause once we were alone. I couldn't believe he was on stage with those skeezas. I didn't want any of them touching him. I didn't care if they were entertainers. I could only imagine one of those skanks slipping Ronald their numbers on a sneak tip, while everyone watched them shake their hips and rub their tits on my man. I wasn't stupid. I played along and walked straight to the stage.

Ronald stood holding the microphone. I couldn't figure out why he still had it. I thought to tell him to give the man back his shit. But that didn't happen. Ronald had more to say. I was hoping the announcer didn't ask for it back. I couldn't stand watching two people fight over a damn microphone. Ronald wasn't even part of the act. When I walked up, he put the microphone back to his lips and faced me.

"Baby," he said, while getting down on one knee.

I looked down at him.

"I want you to know how much I love you. I promise to fill every day of your life with romance. Accept me as your euphoric treasure as I continue cherishing the precious jewel I found in you. I love you. Let's spend our lives together. Deloris will you marry me?"

I stopped breathing. How dare Ronald put me on the spot like this? What was I going to do with a husband? A woman like me didn't just settle down overnight and decide she wanted to cater to a man. I thought for sure this was the end of the thing I had going with Broadway Fatal. Ronald didn't even know what I did for a living. I was closing up shop but was I ready to do it for my relationship? If something were to happen financially, I knew he was strong enough to support me. Ronald had his own money but getting married would have meant I would be forced to make changes with my life, and not make them at my leisure. Living my lavished lifestyle would also have to change. Was I ready to do that? Could I love Ronald as much as he loved me? Would he expect me to get pregnant and have his babies? What about my cute figure?

But, why say no? He was fine. He was intelligent. He was good to me and he definitely brought it in the bedroom. This was more than I could ever say about any other man I dealt with in the past.

I looked at the five carat ring Ronald held in his hand, then looked in his eyes and said, "Yes Baby, I will marry you."

The crowd cheered.

When we kissed, the hula dancers danced around us. I ignored them.

Chenoa
Chapter Nineteen

Love Spell

I guess Deloris wasn't the only one with a surprise. I walked inside of the room after the luau. The fragrance of flowers filled the air. Not just any flowers, but bright red anthuriums. I had to give Sean credit for his choice of flowers. They were probably the most romantic flower in Hawaii. These flowers were shaped like hearts with yellow arrows piercing through the center. Heart shaped peddles were positioned perfectly on the floor and led to the Jacuzzi. They floating in hot drawn water with fluffy suds that covering the edge of the surface.

I didn't want to presume I would be sleeping naked, so I gathered a night shirt and panties from my luggage just in case. I walked back into the powder room and undressed. I removed my costume jewelry and my halter. I slipped out of the wrapped printed skirt and thong panties I was wearing. Sean stood at the door intently watching. I was nervous with him seeing me naked for the first time, but I kept moving. I stepped into the Jacuzzi, sat down and let out a sigh of relief.

Once my body relaxed, I closed my eyes, lay back, and rested my neck on part of the bath cushion that surrounded the tub. When I looked up at Sean, I was reminded of how hot he really was. His chocolate colored skin was gorgeous. With his eyes focused on me, he pulled his shirt over his head and exposed the hairs on his torso that led to his manhood. I looked forward to encountering it soon. I thought his plan was to join me in the tub, but when he decided not to remove his pants, I wondered what his next move would be.

"How does the water feel?" he asked, while walking over then kneeling down.

"It feels great. Aren't you gonna join me?" I asked, shocked at myself for saying that out loud.

"Soon," he answered.

Sean slowly reached into the water and located each of my thighs. When his strong fingers grasped my legs, he used them to lift me up. My butt was sitting on the rim of the Jacuzzi.

I looked at him.

"Relax baby you seem tense," he said, still holding both of my thighs with his hands.

I relaxed my muscles as he slowly propped my legs opened. I flinched a little, but instantly convinced myself there wasn't anything I needed to feel embarrassed about.

"You are so beautiful," he said, while looking at the Brazilian wax that I let Deloris talk me into getting. "Do you mind if I taste it?"

I nodded and gently rubbed on his bald head. He moved in closer. He worshipped and deeply explored my vagina with his tongue. I couldn't control the constant trembling that generated through my legs. He held onto them. My inner walls sensationally throbbed. It released juices that dripped a flavored substance that Sean tastefully enjoyed. My body yearned for more and Sean was ready to give it to me.

"Are you ready for me?" He asked, while looking up at me and licking his lips.

"Yeah, I'm more than ready."

"Let's move this to the other room then."

He grabbed a towel and dried me off, then placed another one on the floor so I wouldn't slip.

Sean didn't wait for me to undress him. He guided me to the bed and unbuckled his pants. The condoms I had in my suitcase remained where I left them. He entered me without one. With each stroke, he caressed and stimulated my clitoris. It went berserk. All night, his shaft remained stiff with its own persistence and determination. Sean gave my body a workout that could put Bally's Total Fitness out of business.

Deloris
Chapter Twenty

Fantasy Island

Ronald made sure I was enjoying myself. We had two days left and I wanted to stay for at least another week. He registered us for more exertions. We took a helicopter ride and toured the island. From our view, most of the beaches were crowded with people. They looked like ants, until the pilot brought us closer. The jet skis and boats made spiral designs in the water while the surfers were either waiting or riding the ocean waves. As we flew over the mountains, the trees stood tall and hid the waterfalls that poured into pools and streams. Chenoa didn't enjoy the view at all. She buried her head in Sean's chest and held on tight. I thought she was going to break Sean's arm. I figured she would eventually if he continued taking her to high places.

"Chenoa, I don't understand why you keep agreeing to do things that make you uncomfortable. You know you're afraid of heights and everybody else knows it, too," I said, rolling my eyes at Sean.

"She won't get over her fear if she doesn't face it. She needs to fight through it," Sean said.

"Fight through it? She's torturing herself and giving me a fucking headache."

"Deloris, calm down," Ronald said, gently patting my knee. "She's a grown woman. She knows what she wants to do. She doesn't need you questioning her actions."

"She doesn't need him putting her up to do crazy shit like this. I didn't come all the way to Hawaii to watch my sister torture herself. She's ruining our trip."

"She's not ruining our trip," Ronald said.

"Well, he's ruining it then."

"Is everything okay," the helicopter pilot asked, looking back at us.

"Calm it down, Deloris," Ronald said. "Yes sir, everything is fine."

"Why in the fuck would she stay in the damn penthouse and take a helicopter ride if she's afraid of heights. This is the dumbest shit I'd ever heard," I said, while looking out of the window.

"That enough, Deloris," Ronald said, and gave Sean an apologetic look. Chenoa kept her eyes closed and continued holding on to him.

I couldn't believe I was actually engaged. Ronald wanted to spend the rest of his life with me. I felt like the luckiest woman in the world. Most women dreamt of finding the right man to settle down with. I was in shock. I guess I'd never had anyone love me at the magnitude that Ronald had. I was a little concerned. I hoped I wouldn't break his heart. I was holding on to a secret as if my life depended on it. At least I thought it had. Telling Ronald about my illegal business wasn't an option for me, but there was the chance of him finding out from a big mouth jealous person that wanted to get back at me for God knows what. This kind of shit made me wonder if people really knew everything about their mate in other relationships. I couldn't imagine letting my left hand know what my right hand was doing all of the time.

My sister was very happy for Ronald and me. The minute Ronald placed the ring on my finger she began asking questions about the wedding plans. The wedding was the last thing on my mind. I needed to get used to the idea of sharing my space and actually living with someone. I thought I made the right decision by saying yes, but we had a few things to work on. In the past, Ronald showed jealous and insecure behavior. I hoped because of our engagement, he would feel more confident with our relationship. Then again, I questioned if he could deal with someone who had such a strong personality as I did. I would have hated getting married and then divorced months later.

The next day the submarine ride made my stomach sick. Chenoa seemed to enjoy this exertion. I hated it. I wanted to see a few killer sharks or whales, but instead saw turtles and some exotic fish. These were some of the same boring sea creatures we saw when we snorkeled and went scuba diving. I couldn't wait to get out of the submarine. I felt claustrophobic being under the water, closed up, and not having much space to move around.

The following day was much better. We had a close encounter experience with dolphins. I thought extorting animals was the cruelest thing ever. Taking animals from the wild and forcing them to perform for financial gain was definitely a selfish act humans did that I didn't appreciate. I was surprised because the dolphins seemed happy. I didn't think they were harmed in any way when I watched how they were being trained. The trainers invited us in the water. We rubbed on the dolphin's bellies and held on to their fins when they pulled us. We even received a few kisses. I found that interesting. I enjoyed this exertion the most, until later I realized how I had easily lost focus of the brutality that happened behind closed doors that I never saw.

We kept busy in Hawaii. It was truly the "Fantasy Island." The food tasted great, the weather was beautiful, and the people were nice. One important fact that I appreciated about Hawaii was how the island was free of any poisonous snakes or insects.

Things were going great, until my sister Chenoa received the call.

Chenoa
Chapter Twenty One

No News is Good News

I was totally hooked on Sean. I was a woman before I met him but was officially transformed. I felt mature and my body felt amazing; it was under Sean's rejuvenating command. I couldn't stand the thought of being apart from him. I wanted him to consider moving in with me. I figured he was probably tired of sharing his apartment with his roommate, anyway. I also wondered what my sister would say about us living together in the house she bought for Demetri and me. I didn't care. I wanted to keep him close and have twenty-four hour access, even though he still had an important job that kept him busy.

We were having a great time in Hawaii, until I received a phone call from my mother. NaDariah and her husband had dropped Demetri off at her house. Instantly, I went into panic mode. I wondered if everything was okay with my baby. My mother reassured me that Demetri was fine. NaDariah needed her to keep him until I returned. She was very upset and needed this favor from my mother. My mother wasn't normally the type who'd babysit without complaining, so I wanted to get back home to my son without being a burden for too long. Before dialing NaDariah's phone number, my cell phone rang. It was NaDariah's phone number but on the other end was a man asking to speak with me.

"Hello," I said, answering in a hurry.

"May I speak with Chenoa, please?" the man on the other end asked.

"This is Chenoa. Who is this?"

"This is NaDariah's husband, Troy. We need to talk."

"Is everything okay? Where is NaDariah and how is she? Is the baby alright?"

"Yeah, I think everything is going to be alright once we meet and talk. I hear you're out of town? When will you be coming back?"

"Can I speak to NaDariah?" I asked, wondering why this stranger was calling my phone and not telling me anything.

"NaDariah isn't feeling well at the moment. I'll have her call you later. Do you think we could meet tomorrow downtown at Trumbull Kitchen around six p.m.?"

"Meet you tomorrow around six?" I asked, and looked at Sean while covering the speaker with the palm of my hand and waiting for his input.

"Look Chenoa, I understand that we've never met and this phone call may seem awkward or weird, but there are some things that are important that you and I need to discuss."

I didn't know what to say to NaDariah's husband. He wouldn't let me speak to her. I didn't recall her ever mentioning anything about her husband physically or mentally abusing her. I wondered why he was calling instead of her. Why was NaDariah so upset? Did they have a fight? I was curious to hear what her husband had to tell me, but I wanted to speak with NaDariah first.

I agreed to meet Troy the next day at six. Whatever he wanted to tell me must have been important. NaDariah gave me her word that she would look after Demetri. I didn't want to think my friend intentionally let me down. When I told Sean what was going on, he was ready to leave Hawaii, too.

"When we get back, I'm going to meet with NaDariah's husband."

"For what? Did he tell you what the problem was?"

"No, he just said he needed to speak with me about something?"

"Well I'm going with you. I hope he don't think you supposed to meet with him alone. He could be some crazed maniac for all we know."

"You don't have to go. I'll be okay."

"Yeah, right. You can forget that. You're not going alone."

The party was over for us. I packed our clothes as Sean and Ronald made the arrangements for us to leave. Even though Hawaii was beautiful, my first priority was to Demetri. Deloris felt the same way. She was packed and ready to go before we were even certain that we were going to catch an early flight. She didn't like the idea of NaDariah's husband calling my phone, either, especially without giving any explanation.

Soon as we arrived back home, we drove straight to my mother's house to pick up Demetri. Demetri and my mom were sitting in the living room watching TV. I felt relieved seeing my baby boy in one piece. His bright hazel eyes lit up the moment I walked through the door. After he ran to my arms, I felt guilty and decided not to take any more long trips without him.

"Hey mommy's little man. Have you been a good boy?" I asked Demetri, while giving him a tight squeeze.

He shook his head and returned the affection.

"What did NaDariah say when she dropped the baby off?" I asked my mom, while still hugging Demetri.

She was watching TV in a daze and didn't answer me.

"Did NaDariah and her husband give a reason for dropping Demetri off?" I asked again when she looked at me.

"No, they didn't give a reason," she responded, but it was obvious she wasn't all there.

What's the matter?" I asked her and let Demetri go.

"Uh, I'm just worried about Pooler and Trinity."

"What happened?"

"Her house burned down yesterday. Pooler left a cigarette burning and it caught onto the rug."

"What?"

"By the time the fire department showed, her house was fully enflamed. She lost everything. Trinity did, too," she said and looked down at the floor where Demetri was playing with a taiko drum I bought for him.

"You know what. That's what she gets chain smoking those damn cancer sticks," Deloris chimed in after ending a phone call she was having.

My mother rolled her eyes at Deloris and walked to the kitchen to get Demetri's left over snacks for me to pack. Deloris and Ronald followed her. I was glad I picked Demetri up when I had. My mother didn't need any added drama.

While half folding Demetri's clothing and stuffing them inside of his bags, I tuned in to what a reporter on the evening news was saying.

"The body of a missing school teacher was found today floating in the Connecticut River. The family has been contacted and he was identified as Tyler Smith of Duke High School. Investigators believe Smith was the victim of a homicide."

My heart started racing when Mr. Smith's picture flashed on the TV screen. My eyes scanned the room to see if I was the only one who was getting ready to have a nervous breakdown. Deloris was showing my mother her new ring while Ronald told his version of the proposal. Sean was outside putting Demetri's toys and booster seat in the car, so he didn't hear the report.

When Sean came back inside, I tried calming myself but it was evident that something was wrong. My lips trembled. Sean grabbed my hands and guided me to the couch. He let one of them go but held onto my wrist and checked my pulse.

"Are you okay? What's going on?" he asked.

Everyone else came in from the kitchen to my rescue.

"She's probably sick from the plane ride," Deloris said then glanced at the TV.

"Yeah, I am. Can someone get me a glass of ginger ale or something? I'm feeling a little dizzy," I said.

"You need to rest, Chenoa. I told you not to torture yourself in Hawaii," Deloris said and cut her eyes at Sean.

"She'll be okay," Sean said, looking back at Deloris with annoyance.

"I'll take the baby home with me. Just go home and rest," she said.

Ronald went outside and put Demetri's things inside of the car that he and Deloris were driving.

I was mentally drained. A lot happened while we were away. NaDariah was having issues with her husband, which somehow concerned me. Aunt Pooler's house had burned down. And Mr. Smith was murdered. I was having problems with processing everything. I wanted to focus on one thing at a time. I thought about the meeting I was going to have with NaDariah's husband.

I replayed events with NaDariah that could have caused problems with her marriage. I was hoping her husband wasn't upset with her for bringing me to poetry night. I wanted to see Sean again. Actually, she was more anxious than I about going. I wondered if he was the kind of husband that got jealous and preferred his wife to stay at home. He probably didn't like her hanging out. But, he lived in D.C., so I didn't think it was fair for him to expect her to not have a social life as long as she wasn't disrespecting him. Other than that, I couldn't think of anything else that could possibly upset him that pertained to me. I'd known her for almost a year and had grown very close. We shared secrets and never had she mentioned cheating on her husband. I assumed the baby she was carrying was his.

Don't Let the Door Hitcha

C oming home sucked. NaDariah spoiled everything. My mother couldn't tell us shit when we stopped by her house. I couldn't wait to find out her story. I thought she would have drilled NaDariah and her husband when they brought Demetri to her. I appreciated her for not making a big ordeal about watching him, though. She was probably too busy focusing on the traumatic fire that Aunt Pooler and Trinity had. She needed a favor and asked me to call her when I made it home. This was something I didn't have a problem with doing, especially when she didn't cause Chenoa any stress by unexpectedly watching her own grandson.

As soon as I opened the door, I put my bags down then plopped down on my couch. I was relieved for making the decision to clean my house before leaving for the trip. Everything was in its rightful place. I didn't have much to do, so I chilled out. Ronald searched through his bags for something to change into and then took a shower. He must have felt more comfortable with me. Normally, he would have asked before jumping into my shower. I hoped he didn't take long because I'd made arrangements to meet Brandy so we could get back to business.

The vacation was over and because I had Demetri and business to tend to, I wasn't planning on giving Ronald my undivided attention anymore. I was hoping after he showered, he would find something else to get into other than hanging around. I wanted to hustle up and replace the money I spent from the heavy shopping I did in Hawaii.

While waiting for Brandy, I fixed Demetri something to eat, located his favorite DVD, *Shrek*, and loaded it into the player for him to watch. I figured the movie would keep him occupied for a couple of hours. When I attempted to bring my luggage in the bedroom, Ronald was coming out of the bathroom. He was half dressed, wearing a pair of boxer shorts and a wife beater. He must have thought we were still on vacation and was in a playful mood. He walked directly to me, lifted me up, and threw me onto the bed. He laid on top of me. My mind was only on making money. I didn't find him hard to resist. I was a hustler and hustlers always thought about making money, even when they didn't need it. Ronald kissed my neck and the doorbell rang.

"Who is that?" Ronald asked and then rolled off of me.

"Oh, that must be my co-worker," I nonchalantly answered.

"Your co-worker? Deloris, we just got back from vacation."

"I know but the store in having a fashion show and they need me to work."

"We are supposed to still be in Hawaii. How are you working today?"

"Well, I'm not really working. They need me to match some color shades to the clothing the girls are going to be wearing."

"Match colors shades for a fashion show? That's crazy," he said, while putting on his clothes.

"I know baby, but why not? I'm home. I might as well make a little money."

"All money ain't good money, Deloris. You need to be spending time with your man."

"Baby, money is money. I'm not going to be long. We'll have time to spend tonight."

"Alright. I'm gonna swing by my crib for a few. I need to check to make sure things are in place over there," he said and then headed for the living room where Demetri was.

When I opened the front door, Brandy stood there with another chick that looked just as bad as she did. Brandy's hair was pulled back in a sloppy ponytail. I'd always known her to wear a fresh wrap. Her skin was all broken out and her eyes had dark bags under them. She looked as if she hadn't slept for days. I didn't bother inviting them in. I stepped outside of the door to find out what her problem was.

"What's up Brandy?" I asked, while sizing up the other chick and waiting for a response from Brandy.

"Um, you asked me to bring you the stuff right?" she asked, while looking confused.

"Who the fuck is this Brandy?"

"Naw, she's cool. She's been helping me out. Ya know, it's been kinda hard tryna get all dis shit mysef," she said, and wiped her nose with her hand.

"Excuse me but I need to talk to Brandy alone for a minute," I said and looked toward the car hoping this chick would jump her ass in it and break.

"Ummm Yo, go get in the car for a minute I'm comin'," Brandy said. She looked embarrassed after telling her friend she couldn't be a part of the conversation. Her new partner walked away and got inside of the car.

"Bitch, don't you ever bring nobody to my fuck'n house! How the fuck I know she's not 5-0 or sumthin'," I said, hoping Ronald didn't hear me.

"Naw she cool. I'm tellin' you, Deloris, she straight," she said and glanced at the car.

"Fuck Dat! I'm not touchin' none of dat shit!" I said, trying hard to keep my voice down.

"Aight look. Imma drop her off and come back."

"Naw, hell fuckin' naw! I'll get back with you," I replied, changing my tone and dialect when I heard Ronald turn the door knob from inside of the house.

"Hey Baby, you leaving?" I asked.

Ronald looked at me and glanced over at Brandy. Her eyes lit up when he looked at her.

"Yeah, I'll be back later," he said, puckering his lips to kiss me.

I puckered mine and gave him a peck on the lips.

"I'll be here," I said.

I didn't bother introducing them. I watched Ronald get inside of his car and pull off. I walked back inside of my house. Brandy was still standing at my door after I slammed it in her face.

Chenoa
Chapter Twenty Three

Lies and Deceit

As Sean and I approached the front of the restaurant to meet NaDariah's husband, we realized we had arrived early. There were a few parking spaces that quickly filled up. Sean pulled into one of them. I wasn't familiar with this restaurant. It attracted professionals working in Corporate America. The restaurant was located next a few prominent insurance companies, so most of the customers dressed conservatively.

Sean agreed to wait inside of the car until after I met with NaDariah's husband. He felt better about it because the parking space he found was near the front entrance. He was able to keep a close eye on me. He turned off the car, and I got out.

When I walked through the revolving door of the restaurant, I didn't know who to look for. I didn't recall NaDariah describing her husband nor had I noticed any family photos when I visited her home. I must have looked out of place standing in the middle of the floor in the lounging area of the restaurant because the hostess walked up to me.

"Welcome to Trumbull Kitchen. May I help you find a table?" the hostess asked.

"Yes, I'm meeting someone here," I said, looking around for a man seated alone.

"Is his name, Troy?" she asked with a smile.

Yes, I answered and then followed her to a table in the corner of the restaurant.

I was anxious to hear the important news NaDariah's husband had to tell me. I was uneasy meeting with my best friend's husband without her. I tried calling her several times but was unable to reach her. Showing up at her house unannounced was out of the question. I certainly didn't want to lose my friendship with NaDariah, but I needed to know why she hadn't contacted me. She didn't tell my mother what was going on when she dropped my baby off, either. I was completely clueless. I wanted an explanation.

As I casually walked to the table, I glanced toward the window to make sure I was still in Sean's view. NaDariah's husband stood up and held his hand out. He looked intimidating because of his size. He could have been an NFL football player. His glasses hid his dark brown eyes and sat on his full figured nose that reminded me of his daughter's. His thick and beautiful black mane was pulled back in a ponytail with locks that seemed highly maintained. His face was bare and his butter-colored skin was smooth. When our hands met, they were soft and showed no indication of belonging to a hard working construction worker.

"Hello Chenoa, I'm Troy. Pleased to meet you," he said.

"Hi," I said, unsure if I was pleased to meet him.

"Thank you for coming under such dubious circumstances. Please, have a seat. Would you like something to drink?" he asked with a smile and looking less intimidating.

I sat down.

"Yeah, I'll have a Sprite soda," I replied, while looking up at the waitress standing at our table before leaving to get the drinks.

"This meeting is very awkward for me," he said, while removing his glasses and rubbing his eyes with both hands.

I waited for him to get his thoughts together.

"Well, the reason why we're here is because there are a few things we need to discuss about my wife. I am a pharmaceutical representative and it is very seldom when I'm at home. Sometimes I'm away for months at a time attending conferences. When I came home a few days ago, I noticed a list of names that NaDariah left on the kitchen counter for her baby shower," he explained, watching my reaction. "I assume you were hosting it because NaDariah doesn't have any other friends, at least any that I've heard her mention lately. So, when the opportunity presented itself, I used her cell phone and called you."

"Yes, I was going to give her a baby shower," I said, trying to figure out where he was going with this meeting and wondering when he became a pharmaceutical rep when he was supposed to be a construction worker. I was confused.

"Why don't you tell me how you and NaDariah met?" he asked, while watching my puzzled expression that I was trying to put back together.

"Long story, but we met at a psych clinic. Why?"

"See, here's the thing. I needed to speak with you because I wanted to save all of us some embarrassment. My wife suffers from a condition called Antisocial Personality Disorder. She was diagnosed with it when she was younger. Because of this disorder, she pathologically lies and can also become very delusional at times," he said, while the waitress brought our drinks.

"So, what are you telling me? She seems outgoing to me," I said, and looked up at him while taking a sip from my straw.

"Chenoa, when people think of antisocial behavior, it is often misunderstood for being unfriendly or withdrawn. Individuals, like my wife, who suffer with this disorder are deceitful, compulsive liars, and often con others just for personal gain or pleasure. I don't know why you were at the mental health clinic, but my wife was there to receive treatment. Working in pharmaceuticals, I've tried finding affordable medications her. We haven't been successful with any of her medications. Her body rejects them, so she tries different ones. This is her reason for being at the clinic."

"I don't understand. She is like the best mother and friend..." I said, still confused.

"It is unfortunate that my daughter is subjected to this situation. More times than none, when NaDariah is having occurrences, we have problems finding individuals to care for her. NaDariah has never done anything to harm our daughter. She's good with keeping herself under control, which is why I've been okay with my traveling schedule."

He took a sip from his drink, his hand shaking slightly.

"I sincerely apologize if I ruined your trip, but I didn't feel comfortable with NaDariah taking care of your son. This is why we dropped him off at your mother's."

"How is she going to take care of the new baby when she needs help with the one y'all have?" I asked, while struggling with wrapping my brain around the fact my only friend was crazy.

"There is no new baby, Chenoa," he said and looked down. "She made the whole thing up. She was never pregnant."

"What?" I asked, trying to pick my mouth up off of the floor.

"NaDariah isn't pregnant," he repeated. "Tamara told me that her mother had been stuffing her clothing so she would appear to look pregnant. She said it was a secret between her and her mother that she evidently couldn't keep to herself and I'm glad she didn't. When I found the guest list, I needed to call you."

"Wow, I don't know what to say. How could she lie to me like this?"

"NaDariah was diagnosed with this disorder for quite some time, Chenoa. Something happened while she was in high school. She was never the same after that."

"What happened?"

"I'll let her tell you," he said.

"I'm not sure if I want to talk to her. I don't want her telling me anymore lies. I shared a lot with NaDariah. I hope she's not just another person I allowed to play with my emotions."

"I understand how you feel. NaDariah and I have been together since high school. I've loved her ever since we were kids. We've dealt with situations together that have brought us to our knees," he said, without breaking eye contact.

"I'm really pissed off at her."

"I know, but imagine how she feels. She doesn't have many friends. It's hard to keep friends with a disorder like the one she suffers with. Deep down inside, I believe she is a good person. She really likes you as a friend, and would probably do anything for you. I don't think she intentionally hurt the people she cares for. She means well, Chenoa."

Deloris
Chapter Twenty Four

Retire From Work Not the Hustle

C henoa and Sean came and picked Demetri up. They found out NaDariah was a psychotic bitch. I should have known it was too good to be true, to believe Chenoa had found someone to be truly sincere to her. NaDariah's husband told Chenoa she had some type of mental disorder. When Chenoa told me, I immediately disagreed with her diagnosis.

"So, what was the emergency meeting about?" I asked Chenoa when she walked into the house.

Sean waited in the car.

"Well, NaDariah's husband said she was sick," she answered, and sat down on the couch.

"Sick from what? Did she miscarry or something?" I asked, trying to sound concerned.

"No, he said she was mentally ill," she hesitantly said.

"Mentally ill? Chenoa, what are you talking about?"

"He said she was diagnosed with Antisocial Personality Disorder."

"What the fuck is that?"

"I don't know, Deloris," she said with a sigh. "He said her illness makes her tell lies and stuff like that."

I just looked at her.

"He said she wasn't pregnant. She made the whole thing up."

Tears ran down my sister's face.

"You know what. That bitch don't have no antisocial shit going on. She wants her husband's attention because he's probably out there fucking all kinds of women while he's so called, 'away on business.'"

"Please. Not now, Deloris."

"How much money did you spend on that nutcase anyway?"

"I bought a few gifts, but I can return them. I'm not concerned about that. I just want to make sure my friend is alright."

"That bitch is fine. She knows exactly what she doing."

Chenoa gathered Demetri's things together and left. I was hoping she wasn't planning on trying to help this pathetic chick when she still had her own issues to deal with. All along, I was concerned about Chenoa depending on NaDariah for her transportation and babysitting favors. It seemed to me that NaDariah needed Chenoa more than I realized.

The next day, I received a call from my mother. I was reminded how I didn't call her like I said I would. Aunt Pooler needed me to help fund Trinity's wardrobe that she lost in the fire. I told her I would because that was the right thing to say. But, I wasn't funding anything. If Trinity needed clothes, she was going to work for them just like everybody else. I was all for helping family, but I wasn't giving away shit, especially to Trinity and her trifling ass mother.

It was Saturday which meant the stores were crowded and busy. This was a good day for Brandy to work. I was desperate, so I called her and arranged for us to meet again. I hoped to receive the merchandise from her that she tried giving me a few days prior. I made a reservation to meet at a nearby hotel close to her apartment. She wasn't coming back to my house, not after the last stunt she pulled. Messing around with her was risky, but she was still dedicated when it came to getting the merchandise and collecting her share of the money. I was still willing to take a chance with her, even knowing she wasn't her old self. She allowed whatever drug she indulged in to control her mind. Brandy wasn't in business for herself anymore, so pushing hard to get money for drugs was her main focus. I figured she needed the money to support her habit, more than she wanted it to better her life. I couldn't get hooked on worrying about Brandy's issues, though. My main priority was making sure she didn't grab a hold of my leg while sinking. I believe this would have happened soon if I wasn't ready to release her.

After making arrangements to meet Brandy, I called my mother to let her know where to have Trinity meet me. Trinity didn't have a problem with the plan. She didn't have two nickels to rub together, nor did she have any support from the girl, Nikki, or any of her other so-called "friends" she dissed my sister for. But, that was water under the bridge. Chenoa had it going on with her new job. She lived in a house and had a car and a new man. She wasn't sweating any incident involving Trinity or her mother. I figured I should reach deep and put it all behind me, too.

Once I was settled in the hotel room, I turned on my laptop and searched the database for items going on sale. I knew to tell Brandy which items to stay clear of because once those items were marked to go on sale, without a receipt, I wouldn't get the full refund for it. I hoped Brandy wouldn't be too scatter-brained to comprehend the information I was ready to give her. And, being Trinity's first time going out with her, I needed the old Brandy I used to rely on.

When Trinity and Brandy arrived, Brandy handed me the merchandise she collected that I refused to take at my house.

"Deloris, you do understand that you set us back a few days, right?" she said, looking more sober than usual.

"Set us back? Look Brandy, I'm not trying to fight with you today. Just give me the shit so I can get us some damn money," I said, trying to be as calm as possible. I didn't want Trinity thinking we weren't good business partners or not in control of what we were doing.

"I was just sayin'."

"Sayin' what Brandy? Why you didn't have your girl that you brought to my house clean these damn clothes for you, then? You wanna know why," I asked, while Brandy stood looking dumb founded. "Cuz you can't find nobody that can do this shit like me. Like I said, let's just forget about it and move on."

She continued taking the clothes she previously stole out of the bags for me to see them.

"Hand me those boxes over there, Trinity, so I can lace them up real quick. We don't have a minute to waste," I said, grabbing the aluminum foil and pushing the clothes aside to work on later.

Trinity handed me two department store bags that held four boot boxes inside. I brought them with me for Brandy and Trinity to use.

I wanted them to get on their way, so I laced the boxes with foil. While I was getting the boxes ready, Trinity studied me as if it were a lesson that she could cram before a big test. Little did she know, learning this lesson took knowledge and skills that was only learned through life experiences. This shoplifting thing was about doing what I felt I needed to do at any cost. I was going to make sure I kept the finest clothes on my back. Growing up, my father took care of everyone else's children but his own. I would never depend on anyone else to clothe me, but I was ready to change and take care of myself the legal way. I had a fiancé. I cared about Ronald. This was going to be the last time I jeopardized my freedom. I didn't feel guilty about the stolen goods or give a shit about the retailers, especially knowing they wrote off the financial damage at the end of the year, anyway.

I briefed Trinity on the plan and reassured her that she was in good hands. I told her Brandy had a clean criminal record to make her feel better, but as far as I was concerned, her record wasn't squeaky enough.

Brandy being the crook she was thought I didn't notice her checking out Ronald when she came over to my house. I was going to be the one to put an end to her sticky fingers.

As for Trinity, she was a fool thinking I would sincerely do anything for her. I told her I would deal with her. She thought I forgot the day she got flip with her mouth when I picked Chenoa and Demetri up from school. Not to mention, her and her mother humiliated me at Chenoa's shower. Trinity was considered the golden child for many years. I was putting an end to her polished reputation. Thanks to me and my prepping skills, I purposely missed a section when I laced the boxes so neither one of those bitches would return home from the mall. I was through.

When Brandy and Trinity left for the mall, I was almost ready to check out of the hotel room. I covered my ass. I made two phone calls. The first call was to Uncle Charm. I wanted to make sure his friend deactivated and deleted the database connections from the department store to my server. This was in case Brandy decided she wanted to use her head and pull me in with Trinity and her. I disposed of all of my detaching materials and got rid of the clothing that needed detaching. And then I dialed up Uncle Charm.

"Hey Unk," I said.

"What's up? You ready?" he asked.

"Yeah, tell her to pull the plug. I'm done," I said, trying to be as direct as possible without giving too much information, while I continued packing up all the things I needed to get rid of. Plus, I didn't want him to know that Trinity was involved with this last trip. She was one of his nieces, too. He wouldn't appreciate my plan.

"Yeah aight. Look Deloris, we need to discuss that thang with Chenoa."

"I know. Thanks for everything."

"Aight, hit me back later."

"Okay, later."

The other call was to my masseuse. I needed a Swedish massage. Since I was getting rid of all the unwanted drama in my life, I figured why not cleanse the unwanted toxins from my system, too. After receiving my massage, I stopped by a nearby Baskin Robins for a scoop of Chocolate Chip Ice Cream. I didn't like eating ice cream when I was depressed or wanted to give myself a pity party. I only associated eating ice cream with celebrating. I'd killed two birds with one stone. A celebration was in order.

I was definitely making some major changes in my life. I wasn't only thinking of myself this time. My plan was going to help others. I was doing Brandy and Trinity favors. Since Trinity's house burned to the ground, I helped her find a place to live for free. She was going to jail. She didn't need to worry about wearing fancy clothes anymore. The jail house attire only required an orange jumpsuit.

As for Brandy, she didn't need to worry about admitting herself into a rehabilitation facility. The prison had its own free detoxification unit. If she had trouble with kicking her habit, she could probably use the same googly eyes she tried using with Ronald. Maybe she could convince one of the correctional officers to bring something in to help keep the monkey off her back. I didn't care one way or the next. Just as long as she wasn't using those looks trying to get my man's attention anymore.

When I got home, my cell and house phone rang off the hook. I ignored it as I ran the water for my bubble bath. Soon as I attempted to get inside, it occurred to me that some of those calls could have been from Ronald. I checked my missed call list. I wanted to make sure I didn't have a disgruntled fiancé searching for me outside during the day time with a flash light. When I noticed he hadn't called, I proceeding with my pampering rituals. After I finished, I transformed into character. This character was starring in a lead acting role, guaranteeing me an Oscar.

Chenoa
Chapter Twenty Five

Prince Charming

I couldn't blame NaDariah for having a psychotic disorder. It wasn't her fault that she was mentally ill. She should have been glad her husband thought enough of their marriage and our friendship to bring her illness to my attention. I thought it was big of him allowing her to keep some dignity, instead of letting her embarrass herself. It would have been awful helping her cover up that terrible lie.

I wasn't sure and wondered if NaDariah and I could remain friends. Did I want to invest anymore time and energy into our friendship, knowing she had more drama in store for me and anyone else she managed to get close to? On the flip side, NaDariah was my only friend. The good times in our relationship outweighed the bad. She helped me in ways I couldn't imagine. She helped me deal with my English grade and Mr. Smith. She even offered her shoulder for me to cry on after the incident with Lance disrespecting me at the basketball game. She was older and had more experience, so I often took advice from her rather than from Deloris. She was a supportive friend. More like an older sister.

I was afraid of getting hurt by her lies, but wanted to hang in there and give her another chance.

It had been two days since I'd seen Sean. I wanted to give him space and thought I needed a little for myself, too. I decided to spend Saturday with my son. I was scheduled to return back to work on Monday, so I planned to relax for a while after I unpacked the bags that Demetri and I lived out of for the past couple of days.

All day Saturday, I couldn't think of anything or anyone but Sean. I wondered what he was doing. He was such a gentleman. I loved everything about him. With every touch and every kiss, I felt the warmth and gentleness derive from his every being. Sean transferred some of the positive energy to me. I wanted to use this energy to mold upcoming days into productive ones. Before Sean, feeling true love was just made up emotions, but my love for him came from deep within. I thought I felt true love before. I was confused. Pain and sorrow mostly existed. I figured because I was a sensitive person with a fragile heart and the capability of loving even when I hadn't received it in return, my heart would always be the victim of pain. But, I wasn't afraid of love. Love agreed with me, so I claimed it and allowed my heart to embrace a powerful force that invaded my mind, body, and soul.

I longed to see Sean, but my brain wanted me to relax and play it cool until he felt the need to call or visit. My heart wanted me to get dressed and fill the empty space that yearned to see him. I listened to my heart. I got dressed and tried to look my best.

When I checked myself in the mirror, I looked well rested. I was glad we had taken the trip to Hawaii. Sean's magic touch had a lot to do with me rejuvenating, too. I felt great. I was thankful for my tan because my skin was flawless. I didn't need to wear any makeup. I was surprised my tan was still noticeable. My hair was alive, too. I wore it down. Sean liked it that way. I was still trying to build my wardrobe, so it was nice finding a pair of black CJ jeans and a white Chanel top with sandals in my closet. This was another small gift I received from my sister as a graduation gift. I was a little out of my element when I got fully dressed. I wasn't used to dressing flashy but was glad I made the effort.

Once I dressed Demetri, we managed to head to the fire station in my Jag. When Demetri and I pulled up, the firefighters were hanging out in the front of the yard. They were dressed wearing khaki pants and blue T-shirts with the station number logoed on the front. I always thought firefighters looked sexy wearing their firefighting gear, but thought the t-shirts made them look even better.

As I sat in the car and watched them, some of the firefighters played cards, enjoying the music, while others stood around the burning charcoaled grill, indulging in what seemed to be an intellectual conversation. Still seat belted in, my eyes continued to scan the scene as I hoped Sean would spot my vehicle and save me from causing attention to myself. I didn't want to interrupt any of the male bonding taking place. When I saw Sean's truck parked next to the fire trucks, I was relieved knowing my trip wasn't wasted. I got out of the car.

The mood was laid back but I sensed something wrong after I noticed the funny looks the men exchanged when they saw Demetri and I approach them. I was well aware of the risk and the possibility of Sean getting upset by showing up unannounced, but I found it strange that he hadn't called. He usually called every day. When I didn't see him, I figured maybe he wasn't at work. Maybe his truck was parked there because he had lent it to one of his co-workers. Sean always talked about his co-workers as if they were his brothers. I remembered him telling me how firefighters had tight bonds that weren't easily broken. Their relationships were built strictly on trust. They trusted one another because they dealt regularly with life and death situations. Depending on each other was a natural thing for them. The minor stuff like trusting with borrowing a car was petty.

After giving this some thought, I wondered how much Sean loved and trusted me. I trusted him with my life. My heart already belonged to him. I wondered if he knew how I felt about him. My plan was to ask him when I spotted him walking toward Demetri and me. He looked gorgeous as ever wearing his khaki and blue uniform like the others.

"Hey Baby, what you doing here?" he asked, while giving me a friendly peck on the cheek. He gave Demetri the soft drink he was holding in his hand. I didn't answer him.

"Where have you been?" I asked, while looking him straight in the eye.

"Workin'," he said, while glancing back over his shoulder at the other guys.

"You can't call somebody and at least let them know you're alive? I've been waiting for your call."

"I'm sorry baby, it's been crazy-busy around here," he said, while gently intertwining his fingers through my curls like he always does.

"Umm, so when you comin' over, cuz I miss you?" I said, hoping he was willing to leave with me.

"I'll be over there in a bit. We're kinda chillin' taday ya know, Imma kickit here for a while then see you in a few," he said, while rubbing his goatee with his left hand.

I noticed a piece of silver metal as his hand fell to his side.

"What's this?" I asked and reached for his left hand, singling out the ring finger surrounded by a platinum band.

"I've been wanting to talk to you about something, Chenoa," he said nervously, grabbing my arm and leading me back toward my car.

"What the hell is this? Tell me what, Sean! That you're freakin' married?"

A lump I once knew revisited my throat. It served its purpose. It prevented me from speaking like it had in the past. As I tried holding back my tears, my heart stopped beating, confirming that it was no longer whole after breaking into a million pieces. When I looked into Sean's remorseful eyes, I wanted to believe the lie and fairy tale relationship I thought we had. Sean was a married man who was given the opportunity to take advantage of a single young mom.

"Tell me what? I'm listening."

"This isn't the time or place to talk to you," he said, looking around to see if anyone was watching.

"Sean, you need to tell me something, now. You're wearing a wedding band that I've never seen before and you want to wait to talk to me?"

"Aight, let me explain," he said, still holding my arm.

I gave him a few seconds but I didn't hear any words come from his mouth.

"Are you married, Sean?"

"Yeah, but let me explain, Chenoa."

"Explain what, Sean? What do you have to explain? You told me what I needed to hear."

I jerked my arm away from his grip and walked back to my car. I couldn't hold back the tears any longer, they flowed down my cheeks as I lifted Demetri up to place him back into his car seat. I was furious. I saw only red, which had nothing to do with the fire trucks parked in the driveway. All I could hear was Sean's voice in my ear asking me to let him explain.

Once I secured Demetri, I walked over to the driver's side. Sean followed. He was pulling on my arm, hoping I wasn't as eager to leave as I was arriving there to see him. When I attempted to get inside of my car, the tight grip Sean had on my arm burned my skin as I tried jerking away from his hold again. I wanted to hear his explanation but I couldn't think of anything he could possibly say to justify breaking my heart. All I wanted at that particular moment was for him to let go of my hurting arm. I was certain we were causing a scene, but was too embarrassed to look at any of the confused faces that were probably wondering what was going on. But, the only face that concerned me was sitting in the back seat of my car crying. I didn't think Sean cared about his coworkers watching either, but once he heard Demetri's cry too, he let go, leaving his red hand print on my arm. With tears still rushing down my cheeks and begging for Sean to leave me alone, a blue Crown Victoria pulled up next to my car. I figured the car belonged to the captain or chief of the fire department. I thought Sean was in trouble for causing a scene in front of the building, especially the way he backed away from me when he saw them. Two men wearing suits with visible badges got out.

"Is everything alright ma'am?" one of the men asked, while looking at Sean and then my rosy arm.

"Yes, everything's okay. I was just leaving," I said, wiping away my tears and snots.

"We're looking for Sean Hightower. Can either of you tell me where to find him?"

After that question, I figured neither one of the men belonged to the fire department. How could they, when the word detective appeared on their badges?

"I'm Sean Hightower. Can I help you with something?" Sean asked, converting into professional mode.

"Yes, I hope so. My name is Officer Stevens and this is Officer Brown," one officer said, and both of them flashed their badges.

"We need to ask you a few questions pertaining to the death of Tyler Smith."

"I'm sorry officers. I don't know a Tyler Smith," Sean said with relief.

I couldn't take anymore. Before I knew it, I was in my car headed home with my son. I wasn't getting involved with anything that concerned investigating detectives, even if I knew Tyler Smith on a personal level.

When the police came by the station for questioning, I could have helped Sean with his alibi because we were in Hawaii when Mr. Smith was killed. But I figured, why do right by him when he didn't care enough to at least tell me he was in another relationship, not to mention being married. I didn't ask him to share what I told him about Mr. Smith and me to anyone. He was on his own the same way he left me.

I dreaded calling my sister. I was stressed out and hurt. Mr. Smith was dead. I wasn't sure if his death had to do with me or if he harassed other girls and caused them misery, too. I needed someone to talk to. Surely, I couldn't call NaDariah with my problems. She was having some type of mental breakdown and wouldn't answer my calls. I hated the fact that Deloris was the only person I could reach. The last thing I needed to hear from anyone was, "I told you so," which were the first words she said to me when I called.

Deloris
Chapter Twenty Six

Wasted Brandy

After taking my bath that evening, I called my mother to find out her emergency.

"Deloris, I've been trying to reach you for hours," my mom anxiously said.

"What? Is everything alright?" I asked, having some idea what she wanted.

"No, everything isn't alright, Deloris. Pooler called saying Trinity is locked up."

"What? Locked up? What happened?"

"You tell me."

"How am I supposed to tell you anything when this is the first I'm hearing of this?"

"I need you to go and get Trinity out of jail. I don't know what happened but she's being held on a one hundred thousand dollar bond."

"One hundred grand? For what?" I asked, genuinely surprised for the first time in our conversation and not understanding the seriousness of the offense.

"Your friend Brandy pulled a gun on security when they were leaving the store."

"A gun? Brandy wouldn't do anything like that," I said, lying to my mother. There was no telling what her capabilities were in the drug state she was probably in.

"Pooler is saying Brandy tried stealing jewelry and some other stuff."

"Jewelry?" I astonishingly asked, amazed that she would try to pull this.

"Deloris, will you please go and get your cousin out of jail. This is her first offense, so you should be able to bail her out."

"I'm not going to no jail to bail nobody out. Where am I going to get the money for that?"

"It should only cost ten thousand. Don't bail bondsmen only ask for ten percent up front?"

"Only ten thousand? You're saying 'only' like money grows on trees. My money is tied up in real-estate and don't even ask cause I'm not putting my property up for nobody."

"I can't believe you, Deloris."

"Well believe it. I tried helping Trinity and Aunt Pooler," I said, but didn't quite explain what my idea of helping them entailed. "She knew shoplifting would risk Trinity's freedom. Why would she put her daughter out there like that anyway? She's going to have to get out the best way she can. I have to go. Chenoa is calling on the other line."

I clicked over.

The information my mother gave me was music to my ears. For some crazy reason, Brandy tried stealing jewelry. This wasn't her area of expertise. Brandy's ass was strung out. Trinity caught a federal charge because of her. I didn't think they would get into this much trouble. I thought they would be held for a few months then released. They were facing some serious charges that didn't have all to do with me. I had twenty grand to pay the bondsman to get them home. Why would I do that? The situation they were in was even better than I imagined. I wasn't putting myself out for them. Brandy and Trinity knew they were taking risks. That was just a part of the game.

I wasn't going to worry myself about Brandy and Trinity. I was concerned about my sister's situation. It was time for her to suck up all of the little girl shit and become a woman. I heard the whole conversation Sean had with the professor's wife at the graduation. I was sure Chenoa didn't approve of him telling her about what her husband tried to get my sister to do in order to pass his class. I'm sure whatever Chenoa told Sean was told to him in confidence.

After the graduation, I immediately called Uncle Charm and told him what was going on. I wasn't going to let that dirty bastard get away with trying to fuck my sister against her will. Uncle Charm said he would take care of him and he followed through with doing exactly what he said. I wanted the professor dead. I was relieved when they announced his death on the news the day we returned from Hawaii. I heard it but Chenoa didn't think I did.

What was the point of Sean telling the professor's wife? Was this his idea of helping Chenoa's situation? Sean telling the little wife not only made him look like the jealous boyfriend, but also the one with most cause for wanting him dead. Well, I was her sister and was going to be sure to end Mr. Horny Professor by more than just talking to his spouse.

Sean had a lot of explaining to do with the authorities for talking, especially without having the audio tape to back him. Chenoa was so predictable, when I heard Sean mention that the tape existed, I purchased the safe, because I figured Chenoa would keep the tape there. I had the combination. I retrieved and disposed of it before we even left for the trip. If Sean wanted to tell something, he should have started with telling the truth about being married. Did he really think after giving me his address to make travel arrangements for Hawaii, I wouldn't check out his story? I knew he was married before we left for the trip. I figured, eventually, Chenoa would find out for herself. I didn't want her to resent me after hearing it come from my mouth.

"Hello," I said, answering Chenoa's call.

"Hey, can you talk?"

"Yeah, I can talk."

"Are you alone because I need someone to talk to?"

"Yeah, what's up? What's going on?"

"It's Sean."

"I told you."

"He is freakin' married," she said, while retaining the outburst she wanted to release.

"Married?"

"Yeah, Demetri and I just left the station and he was wearing a wedding band. How did I miss that?" she asked.

"I told you I didn't trust him from the start. When I told you to keep your business to yourself you didn't want to hear it. Now look? The man is married with business of his own that you knew nothing about."

She tried silently crying in the phone but I heard her.

"I'll be over in a minute," I told her.

"Okay," she sniffled and hung up.

I'm sure it took a lot for Chenoa to call me with this drama. Instead of heading to my mother's house, I headed to Chenoa's. Supporting my sister was something I needed to do, despite the fact that I could have prevented this all from happening in the first place.

On the way to Chenoa's house, I thought about how much life experiences could change a person. It only took one time for someone to burn me. It didn't make sense giving second and third chances. What was the point? To prove at the end of the day that the results would turn out the same regardless? Maybe Chenoa would be more cautious with choosing her male and female friends. NaDariah turned out being some kind of psychopath and from the start, and Sean had a look in his eye that reminded me of a desperate game show contestant preparing to make it to the final round.

Game always recognized game.

Deloris
Chapter Twenty Seven

Give Some

When I arrived at Chenoa's, the Jaguar was parked in the driveway and a car was parked in front of the house. I wondered if she had company. When she opened the door, her face looked flustered. She was definitely going through changes. I almost felt sorry for her but it was necessary for her to go through changes in order to get past her pain. Why try to mend her broken heart? In order for her to come back strong, she needed to rebuild, start over, and make sure her new heart was sturdy enough to endure the heavy weight that would put its strength to the test again.

I walked inside of the house and sat down on the new leather sectional. The house was quiet so I figured the car out front belonged to the neighbors.

"So, what's this about Sean?" I asked, while my eyes searched the room for my nephew. "Where's Demetri?"

"He's sleeping," she said.

"So, what were you telling me on the phone about Sean?" I asked, while catching a glimpse of the red mark on her arm.

"He's married," she said and sat in the chair adjacent to the one I was sitting on.

"So, what are you going to do about it? I hope you're not planning on still seeing him," I said, wondering where he found the nerve with leaving his hand print on my sister. Maybe I needed to talk to Uncle Charm about him, too.

"No, that's not my plan, but I do love him, Deloris. If I can throw my love for him out of the window so easily then my feelings for him can't be real. Maybe he made a mistake or maybe I pushed too hard."

"That's bullshit, Chenoa. You have to stop letting these no good ass bastards play you and get away with it."

The last thing I wanted Chenoa to do was take responsibility for someone else's faults. I didn't want her to cater to her own low self esteem and then eventually settle with becoming a mistress instead of a wife.

"I wouldn't say he's no good. He tried helping me with a situation I was going through while I was in school," she said, while silencing her cell phone after it rang.

"What situation?" I asked, pretending I didn't know already.

"Don't trip Deloris when I tell you. I know how you can get."

"What situation?"

She looked at me and paused trying to decide if she wanted to tell me. She sighed.

"I was having trouble with my English teacher at school. I was almost failing his class, so I went to him for help with my grade. Well, let's just say he was unprofessional. I told Sean about it and he informed my teacher's wife of the situation. When we came back from Hawaii, I heard on the news that he had been killed. And when Demetri and I were at the fire station, the police were looking for Sean."

"Damn, I'm impressed. I didn't know Sean had big balls like that. He killed somebody for you?"

"How could he? We were in Hawaii when this all happened," she asked, seeming distracted again when her phone rang a second time. She silenced it, so I assumed it was Sean calling.

"He could have something to do with it. Look how he lied to you about being married. I didn't trust him from the start. I knew he was no good."

"I don't think Sean would do anything like that."

"You didn't think he would lie to you about being married and tell your teacher's wife either, but he did."

"Yeah, you're right about that, but I don't think he could kill anyone."

"He had something to do with it, Chenoa. And if they call you in for questioning, you need to tell them everything you just told me."

"Do you think I should also tell them that my sister stole the audio tape from my safe to cover her own behind?"

"What?"

"The tape has been missing for days. You're the only one with the combination to the safe other than myself. I hid the tape there."

"I don't know what you're talking about."

"Yes, you know exactly what I'm talking about. Did Uncle Charm kill Mr. Smith? Because if he did, I'm not framing Sean for it."

"Not framing Sean for it? This is the same man who lied to you about being married. Are you telling me that you would turn your back on me for a piece of dick?"

Chenoa sat on the chair with her arms crossed, refusing to answer the question or her phone when it rang for a third time.

"You are so fucking ungrateful," I said. "If it weren't for me you would still be living in a one-room shack and bumming rides. I've always looked after you."

"What does any of this have to do with you doing things behind my back?"

"Doing things behind your back? It seems that the other people in your life either broke your heart or made you feel as if you weren't worth shit. They've lied to you or tried taking advantage. I've only helped you. Do you think Trinity would be sitting in jail if she hadn't fucked with you?"

"Sitting in jail?" she asked with wide eyes.

"Yes, sitting in jail. She got caught stealing. Thought she was going to use me to help her get new clothes. I rigged the boxes so the store alarm would sound. I fixed her ass good."

"Deloris you are crazy. I don't know what to say to you anymore. You are out of control."

"You're right. I am out of control. Everything I've done, I've done for you. Now I need you to do something for me. Fix this."

"Why would you make me choose? Sean is the man I love and he didn't have anything to do with what happened to Mr. Smith."

"Well, I am your sister. You should never have to think twice about sticking with me. Blood is thinker than water."

"I'm sorry, Deloris. I'm gonna think twice about this one. You need to take your own advice. Blood wasn't thicker than water when you had Trinity arrested."

"Fuck her!"

Chenoa got up off of the chair and left the room to check on Demetri. I couldn't believe her attitude. Thanks to me, she didn't have to worry about any tape or being black mailed anymore. Her best bet was forgetting the ordeal with Mr. Smith even happened. If she chose not to she would be giving her diploma back. Once the school found out her grade was given to her without her earning it, they wouldn't let that shit fly. She would have to take the English class again and her integrity would be challenged at every college she applied to.

Maybe I was wrong giving Chenoa all of those things she hadn't worked for. She seemed okay with living the lifestyle she was living. I'm the one who had a problem with it. I didn't like her living in that cramped apartment, broke as hell, and bumming rides from people. I didn't want that life for my sister. We had the same blood running through our veins. Of course, I expected her to jump on board and protect our family the same way I'd protected her. She couldn't defend Sean. He was the man who lied to her and had broken her heart. But if she decided to defend him, who else would they have to blame for the murder? My guess would have been Uncle Charm or myself. I wasn't the one who murdered Mr. Professor, but I sure as hell had a lot to do with it.

Chenoa walked back in the room struggling to keep Demetri draped over her shoulder, while he slept.

"You know what Deloris? I was trying to give you the benefit of a doubt when I accepted the gifts from you."

"I'm not throwing anything back at your face. I'm just saying you wouldn't have anything if it wasn't for me."

"That isn't true, Deloris."

"Yes, it is true. You would still be confined inside of the house without transportation and you would still be miserable."

"Deloris, I don't need all of this stuff you gave me. Trust me. I will do okay without it."

"What will you drive, Chenoa? Where would you go?"

"You don't have to worry about me anymore. You can have all of your material things back."

"Where are you gonna go? Oh, you're gonna go live with Sean and his wife?"

"Don't worry about it. I'm not going to be living here anymore. I'm out," Chenoa said, and left out of the door with Demetri.

My own sister was just going to walk out on me like that after everything I did for her. She'll be back, I thought.

Chenoa
Chapter Twenty Eight

Take More

That day was supposed to be about me, not Deloris. But, my sister always made everything about her. I think she enjoyed throwing all of the things she'd ever done for me back at my face. After thinking about it all, I realized it had always been her problem with me not living with the luxuries she had. I don't recall ever complaining about not living a lavished lifestyle.

So, for my sister to ease her conscience and make feel better, she showered me with all of those material things. I didn't want to seem ungrateful with my sister's attempt at making my life easier. I was just amazed how selfish a person could be even while being generous. I didn't like the way she assumed I always needed her to come to my recue. She made me feel as if she didn't have any confidence that I could solve some of my problems.

As I drove off with Demetri in the back seat, my cell phone continued ringing. I figured it was Deloris or Sean calling me. I didn't want to speak to either of them. I was fed up. I needed fresh air and a minute to clear my head. When I reached in my purse to turn off the ringer, I noticed I had missed a call from NaDariah. With everything else going on, I didn't have the chance to think about the situation we were going through. My day had already taken a downward spiral. I wasn't sure if I wanted to talk to her, either. But, I figured we should discuss our friendship. I needed her more than ever.

"NaDariah?" I asked when she answered the phone.

"Yeah, it's me," she said.

"I've been trying to reach you but you haven't returned any of my calls."

"I'm sorry, Chenoa. Can you meet me so we can talk?"

"Okay, where are you?"

"I'm at your high school."

"What are you doing at my high school?"

"Just trying to clear my head."

"Okay, I'll be there in a few."

When I pulled up, NaDariah's car was parked next to the custodial building at the edge of the parking lot, which was empty. I parked next to her car. When I looked for her, I almost didn't see her sitting on the grass staring at the building. She wore a gray sweat suit with the hood of the jacket covering her head. Demetri was still asleep, so I rolled his window down. I wanted to be able to hear him in case he woke up. I walked over to where NaDariah was and stopped behind her as she spoke in a low voice.

"This brick house is where it all began."

I kept quiet and sat on the ground next to her.

"I thought his career ended after me," she said and briefly looked at me then back at the building. "But I saw him at your graduation. Saw him coming out of the ladies room. I figured he was still at it."

"You're talking about, Mr. Smith?"

She looked at me and just barely nodded. Her eyes were full of hate. My heartbeat thumped at an uncontrollable rate. Still in her low voice, she continued speaking.

"I was a freshman. He was teaching drama. I always wanted to become a famous actress or a poet. I've loved poetry ever since I could remember."

Tears started pooling in her eyes, rinsing the hate out with sadness.

"I was having trouble remembering my lines. He offered to help me. He'd practice with me after school."

It sounded too familiar to me. I didn't know if I wanted to hear anymore, but I kept listening.

"One day after school, I needed to work on a backdrop for a scene for one of the plays I was in. I needed more paint. He kept it in there," she said, pointing to the janitorial building like she was accusing it.

"He had the keys. He opened it for me. I stepped inside to get the paint. He locked the door."

She started sobbing again. I felt for her. I could have been her. I put my arm around her, while glancing back at my car to make sure Demetri was still sleeping.

"It's all right now. He can't hurt anyone anymore," I tried telling her to calm her down.

"I was so humiliated," she managed to keep speaking through the sobs. "I smelled like his awful cologne. I couldn't stand it. I went home and washed his stink off of me. I scrubbed myself so hard. And when I felt strong enough, I told my mother, but it was too late. She called the authorities. But I waited too long. There wasn't enough proof of what he did. But it was enough to get him fired. My mother wasn't the first to make an accusation."

"Fired?"

"Yeah, they fired him because my mother threatened to sue. A few weeks later, I found out I was pregnant."

"Oh my gosh, NaDariah," I said, holding her tighter as she started shaking.

"There was no way I was keeping a baby at fourteen. I was humiliated and I didn't want to shame my family, so my mother brought me to the clinic."

"NaDariah, I'm so sorry."

"Troy and I didn't get together until the following year. I was pretty messed up. I've been struggling with this for a long time, Chenoa. After Troy and I got married, it took us a while to get pregnant. We were finally blessed with Tamara, though. We've had a hard time conceiving, since."

"Wow, I just don't know what to say."

"Say you'll still be my friend. I'm sorry if I hurt you," she said while looking into my eyes. "I guess I freaked out when you told me that you were having trouble with a teacher. That triggered memories that I worked hard with forgetting. And worse, he was the same man. But, it's all over now, like you said. He can't hurt anyone anymore."

"Yes, it's all over," I said, staring at that brick building. "I'm still your friend. You don't have to worry about that."

After hearing the truth from NaDariah, I had to forgive her. We had a good relationship, just as I thought. She felt bad about lying to me. I wished Deloris did, too. I wanted to tell Deloris so much more, but I couldn't trust her, which was why I had been putting money aside. I saved enough to purchase a used car and rent an apartment.

We could have been a lot closer, if only she was more tuned in with my feelings. I loved my sister and would have never done anything to hurt her. This was why I couldn't figure out the reason she worried so much about me defending Sean instead of supporting her and Uncle Charm. I didn't need to defend Sean, because I knew he was innocent and the authorities would eventually let him go.

And if Deloris had called Uncle Charm before coming to my house, she would have found that Uncle Charm had nothing to do with Mr. Smith's murder, either. My uncle called me after I left the fire station. He was worried that Mr. Smith ended up dead when he didn't do the killing. He was worried about Deloris.

And my sister should have known better. Since when did Uncle Charm do anything for me, anyway? She was Uncle Charm's favorite niece. I was just her sister, which I'm sure wasn't enough to expect being granted equivalent royalties as her, especially not a murder.

Telling Deloris would have made our conversation a lot easier. But, I was still working things out in my head. I didn't want to believe who the murderer was. But, I kept remembering the strange telephone conversation I had while I was in Hawaii. I knew exactly who killed Mr. Smith.

But after hearing her story, I could forgive NaDariah for that, too.

Epilogue

While hanging pictures in my new apartment, I looked out of the kitchen window at the beautiful view overlooking the pool. I couldn't help but think about Sean and how he helped me overcome my fear of heights.

"Who is it?" I asked after hearing a knock at the door.

"It's me, Unk. Open the door."

I set my hammer aside and walked over to the door to open it. I was surprised he was paying me a visit. He was dressed in a suit and tie.

"Hey, Niece. What's goin on?"

"Wow, you look spiffy today," I said with a smile.

"Thanks, I had business to take care of today," he said and kissed me on the cheek. "You're workin' hard."

"I'm trying to get settled in my new apartment," I said and walked back to where my pictures were.

"Oh, aight. I want to talk to you about ya sister."

"Why, what about her?" I asked, while taking up my hammer again. "Look Uncle Charm, I'm trying to live my life drama free. I'm not trying to get caught up with Deloris and her mess again."

I walked back into the kitchen and continued hanging my pictures.

"Naw, Imma little worried about her, ya know," he said, watching me hammer nails into the wall.

"Well you never worry about me," I said, almost catching my finger.

"Niece don't be like dat. I worry about all of my nieces. Where my nephew at?"

"He's in his room watching a video."

"Aight, cool. I wanted to talk to you, Chenoa, because evidently I'm being misunderstood," he said and took off his suit jacket.

"What do you mean?"

"Well, do you remember what happened to your dad when you were young?"

"Yeah, but no one ever wants to talk about it."

"The family tried getting you girls some help when Deloris shot him. I've always wanted the best for y'all. Ya know that right?"

I didn't answer him. I just stood there waiting to hear what Deloris had done this time.

"When Deloris asked me to kill ya teacher, I felt ashamed that I steered her the wrong way. I didn't want her thinking that every time she couldn't get her way that it was okay to off somebody or hurt them. Times have changed. I'm not tryna do no bid off no second hand information."

"I didn't know Deloris came to you."

"You should have come and told me you were having trouble with a grown ass man tryna hurt you. Why did ya sister have to come and tell me that, Chenoa?"

"I don't know. I guess I was afraid."

"You should never be afraid to tell me nothin'. I've always loved my nieces and I love all of y'all the same. Ya hear me?"

"Yes, I hear you."

"Ya sister gonna need some help. She even got Trinity locked up."

"Yeah, I heard."

"I'm not tryna visit none of y'all in jail and I don't want y'all having to visit me. Don't get me wrong. I ain't fa no bullshit. Ya know what I mean?"

"Yes, I hear you."

"Let me go holla at little man then imma have to break."

"Alright."

Uncle Charm went inside of Demetri's room to visit him. While he was visiting, I hung the rest of my pictures and unpacked some of my things. I came across a pair of curtains then walked inside of the living room to hang them. While hanging the curtains, I noticed a fancy car pulling up in the parking lot. I hoped it wasn't Deloris. I wasn't ready to be bothered with her, yet. But as I took a longer look, I wasn't surprised to see Lance and a girl getting out the car. And they were walking toward my building.

I couldn't believe what it took to get Lance to come visit his son. I wasn't surprised but knew that day would be the last time I allowed him to use me as his doormat. I played back in my mind how he left Demetri and I stranded at the basketball game. It was time for me to demand the respect I deserved.

I opened the door before Lance could knock. He stood erect, holding shopping bags in his hands. The girl standing slightly behind him was the same girl I remembered with the bobbed hair cut from the basketball game.

"What are you doing here?" I asked, while giving him attitude.

"Hello to you, too," he said with a phony grin.

"So, you decided to visit your son?" I asked with my body blocking the doorway.

"Yeah, I wanted to call first but I didn't have your number."

"Well, you found my house number okay," I said, looking at the bags he was holding.

"Can I see my son?"

"Not until you give me an explanation as to why you care all of a sudden," I said and watched the girl move to his side. He threatened her with his eyes.

"Oh, Chenoa this is Keisha," he introduced and I acknowledged her.

"Chenoa that was some fucked up shit you did to me," he said.

"Did to you?" I asked, still blocking the door.

"Yeah, did to me. You didn't have to go and have my wages garnished. If you needed money all you had to do was ask."

"I couldn't even get a damn ride from you, Lance, and you're saying all I needed to do was ask you to take care of your son? Well, I don't have to ask you for anything, anymore."

"Yeah, I know. How do you think I found out where you lived? I'm sure you're getting them checks on a reg."

"Yes, I am getting them regularly and your son deserves them."

"No doubt, no doubt," he said, looking me up and down and checking out my expensive outfit. "Now that I'm taking care of my son, can I see him?"

I opened the door and let him in. Keisha followed.

I wasn't going to play with Lance anymore. If he didn't want to step up to the plate and take responsibility for his son, I was going to hit him where it hurt, his pockets. He would have been better off as a passenger at the game. When I told NaDariah that he offered me a ride and left me stranded at the game, she helped me figure out how to gain financial stability for my son. We went to the DMV. I didn't know registering a car was public information. Lance's car was registered in his name. I didn't follow Deloris's plan with staying on welfare, because I didn't need to. When I began working full-time and no longer needed assistance from the state, I had all of his personal information pulled from the DMV, and I reported him to the Child Support Enforcement Agency. He remembered he had a son when the state garnished his paychecks. He wanted to see where his money was going, which was why it didn't surprise me when he showed up at my front door. If he wanted to see his son, he could have done this a long time ago. I never intentionally kept Demetri away from seeing his father.

"Demetri is in his room playing. Have a seat," I said.

Lance put the bags down he was holding and sat down on the couch. Keisha sat next to him and looked around the room at the new pictures I hung of ducks in flight.

"Demetri, come here baby. Somebody's here to see you," I called out, knowing who else was back there, too.

Demetri came running out of his room. He ran straight to me when he saw Lance and Keisha.

"He is so cute. Lance, he looks just like you," Keisha said with her arms opened for Demetri to come to her, but he didn't.

"Come see daddy, Demetri," Lance told him.

He looked at the bag sitting on the floor next to his father and held onto my leg.

"Oh, I bought the baby some things. Let me know how they fit," Lance said, handing me the bag.

"Okay thanks," I said and took the bag. I reached inside and pulled out a stuffed animal and gave it to Demetri.

He was excited to have it, so excited he brought it to show Uncle Charm when he came into the living room to grab his coat.

I wasn't playing with Lance anymore.